THE gargoyle IN MY YarD

The gargoyle
in my yard

Philippa

Dowding

Napoleon

Toronto, Ontario, Canada

Cover art and design by Emma Dolan

Le Conseil des Arts du Canada | The Canada Council for the Arts

We acknowledge the support of the Canada Council for the Arts for our publishing program. We acknowledge the financial support of the Government of Canada through the Book Publishing Industry Development Program (BPIDP) for our publishing activities.

Napoleon Publishing
an imprint of Napoleon & Company
Toronto, Ontario, Canada
www.napoleonandcompany.com

Printed in Canada

MIX
Paper from
responsible sources
FSC
www.fsc.org   FSC® C004071

ANCIENT FOREST ™
FRIENDLY

13 12 11   5 4 3 2

Library and Archives Canada Cataloguing in Publication

Dowding, Philippa, date-
The gargoyle in my yard / Philippa Dowding.

ISBN 978-1-894917-82-7

    I. Title.
PS8607.O9874 G37 2009   jC813'.6   C2009-900684-7

For Sarah and Ben,
who have a gargoyle of their own

PROLOGUE

The year is 1604. It is a long time before our story takes place.

A tall, thin man wearing a long, dusty cloak stands up from his work and surveys the green English countryside before him. It is not his country, but he appreciates that it is a beautiful place nonetheless. He brushes his hands upon his cloak, trying to remove some of the dust. He is covered in dust. Dust is everywhere. In his hair. In his nose and mouth. In the creases of his hands and eyes. This is because he is a stonemason; he works all day long fitting stone together to make buildings and bridges and churches.

Today he is putting the last touches on the restoration of a very old English church. He has been working here for five years, and he will miss this lovely place. There are rolling green hills as far as the eye can see, beautiful old chestnut trees everywhere, and a very pretty little river running beside the church courtyard. The river runs past an ancient statue of a lion, with a regal mane and fierce stone eyes.

As the stonemason stands looking over the small church parapet onto the peaceful countryside he will soon be leaving, he strokes a small statue. He has just created this little statue, something he does at the end of every job he completes. It is his signature. And this statue is his new favourite of all the many, many statues he has carved in his long and illustrious career.

It is a little gargoyle with folded wings and a pouch at its side, perched freely and looking over the churchyard and fields below. As the stonemason pats the gargoyle one last time and turns his back to the church forever, the gargoyle gives a small shudder. And breathes at last.

Chapter One
A New Statue

Katherine looked at her homework piled up on the kitchen table.

"Too much to do," she thought and took another bite of her apple. She munched slowly looking out the kitchen window.

A beautiful fall day was happening outside, without her.

The maple tree against the back fence was glorious with orange, yellow and red leaves gently fluttering to the ground. The warm sun shone on the still-green grass. The fall flowers were in full bloom, and her favourite flowers of all, her mother's award-winning New England Asters, were showing their pretty purple faces to the world.

Her mother and father were really proud of their fall flowers and had the awards to prove how beautiful they were. Katherine had grown up around flowers and knew many of their Latin names: the New England Asters were called "symphyotrichum novae-angliae".

She sighed, tapping her pencil on the table, and took another stab at math problem #6. She read: "Mr.

3

Henry has 3,335 nails and 170 boards to nail onto the fence. If he uses 16 nails for every two boards, how many nails will he use in all? Bonus: How many nails remain unused?"

"Uggh," she said out loud and decided to walk outside to clear her head. She grabbed her apple and said "Come on, Milly," to the pretty calico cat. She let the screen door slam behind her as she escaped the dull world of Mr. Henry and his nails and boards.

Katherine went and sat on the backyard swing, slowly dragging her feet in the grass, the maple leaves falling on her long hair. Her green eyes took in a little statue sitting nearby.

The new garden gargoyle had his back to her a few feet away, with his head in his hands and his wings folded tightly behind his back. He was one of the many garden ornaments Katherine's parents kept in their tiny backyard.

He looked as though he was thinking hard about something. He was sitting on a small pedestal made of stone which had once belonged to a goddess statue, now long gone. This little gargoyle was brand new to their garden, and he was now her favourite.

There were plenty of statues to choose from. Even though their backyard was small, it was definitely full of interesting things to look at. You might say her parents, well, her mother really, were statue-freaks. And they gardened constantly. For such a small piece of land, her father liked to say their backyard got more attention than Casa Loma.

Their garden already had six statues: a little faun

with the body and face of a man and the legs of a goat; a small cherub with an angelic, baby face, perfect wings and a little harp; three bearded, pointy-hatted dwarves; and a water fountain with a unicorn in the middle. The water splashed out of the unicorn's long, curly horn.

But she liked the gargoyle the best. He had a thoughtful sort of face (for a gargoyle) and folded wings that looked leathery and real. He also had a small pouch at his side, bulging with something she couldn't make out.

Katherine wondered what a gargoyle would keep in a pouch like that?

"What do you have in that pouch, Mr. Gargoyle?" she asked. Katherine was reading *The Hobbit* in school and wondered if the gargoyle was anything like a goblin. "Do you have some snails, and wet string and a sharp stone to gnaw? Why I bet ..." she was going to go on, but stopped when she heard her mother call from the kitchen.

"Hi, Katherine! I'm home..."

"Hi Mom!" she yelled back and hopped off the swing. She ran past the gargoyle, dropped her half-eaten apple in the grass, stroked Milly, who was sunning herself on the porch, and disappeared back into the house with a slam of the screen door.

Katherine didn't see what happened next, but Milly did.

Slowly, a small, leathery claw reached out and closed around the apple Katherine had dropped. The gargoyle was hungry.

CHAPTER TWO
THE SIGN OF
THE BROKEN DWARF

That night when Katherine was brushing her teeth, she remembered to ask her dad something.

"Hey Dad, when did we get that new gargoyle?" she yelled down the hall, through foamy toothbrush spit. She spat it out.

"Gargoyle? What gargoyle?" he asked, sounding puzzled as he walked into the bathroom. Her dad was really tall and skinny, with frizzy white hair that made him look kind of like a clown, especially when he was wearing his pajamas as he was now. Her dad was a high school science teacher, and his students liked to call him "Einstein" because he looked a little like that famous scientist.

"Don't tell me your mother bought another garden statue?" he moaned. "What is it this time?"

"A gargoyle. He's really cute, too. For a gargoyle, I mean. And he's real-looking. You know? I mean, you can tell the faun, and the cherub and the dwarves aren't real. And the unicorn is really pretty fake-looking. But the gargoyle has this look on his face, like he's thinking about something really hard. Or maybe he's a little sad. And he's got a pouch bulging with something, but you can't see inside."

Katherine got quiet. "Yeah. He really does look sad about something."

Her dad laughed. "You must have been looking at him pretty hard. I hope he doesn't get into any fights with the dwarves! Gargoyles and dwarves are sworn enemies, you know. They'll fight over nothing and hold grudges for ever. Or almost for ever."

He smiled, leaned down and kissed her on the top of her head.

"G'night, honey. Sleep tight, sweet dreams, don't let the gargoyles bite!" he teased.

"G'night Dad." Katherine yawned as she headed down the hall.

Katherine's bedroom was at the back of the house, closest to the backyard. The tree branches outside her window played a slow game of tag with each other in the gentle night breeze. Katherine sighed and snuggled deep under her covers, glad to be cozy in her own bed, drowsy and happy, ready for sleep.

But she didn't sleep well that night at all. Katherine had fitful dreams of something, or someone, screaming and fighting outside her window. At one point it was as though a lost night creature was banging the tops of the garbage cans together and yowling at the moon.

A few times she dug her head deeper into her pillow and fell back to sleep. Once she rolled over and mumbled "stupid raccoons" before jamming her favourite stuffed bear over her ear to block out the noise.

Milly spent all night sitting in Katherine's bedroom window, looking out into the backyard and growling gently to herself. Once in a while her tail twitched slightly, but otherwise she looked still as a statue. She was watching something very intently.

The next morning, Katherine woke up late for school, tired from a bad night's sleep. When she ran downstairs to grab some breakfast before dashing out the door to school, she didn't even think twice when her mom asked her, "Do you know how the garbage can lids got all over the backyard? Or how one of the dwarves got his nose broken off?"

"Stupid raccoons, they were fighting all night long. Bye!" And Katherine was gone.

Chapter Three
The Chuckle

After such a bad sleep, it wasn't a great day for Katherine.

She misplaced her math book and got in trouble with Mrs. Glean three times, which meant her name went up on the board with a frowning face above it. No matter how hard Katherine tried to get her name and frowny face erased, they stayed there all day.

At three thirty, Mrs. Glean asked her to stay for a few moments to "chat". Katherine had never been asked to stay after school before, except for good things like band practice or to help the little kids get their snowsuits on.

It wasn't that Mrs. Glean was a terrible teacher; in fact, she could be quite helpful and knew a lot about important things, but she always had a cup of coffee in her hands. There was nothing Katherine liked less than stale coffee-breath.

"Katherine," she started, "are you having problems concentrating today for some reason?"

"No, not really."

"Well, if there is some problem you want to talk

about, please feel free to discuss it with me. Your math book will probably turn up, so don't worry about that. But you weren't really yourself today... Is everything all right?"

"Yes, everything's fine," Katherine said. "We just had a loud raccoon fight going on in the backyard last night, and it was hard to sleep, so I'm a little tired today."

"Okay," Mrs. Glean smiled, "that's fine. Let me know if you need extra help with anything."

That was that. Katherine breathed out and slipped out behind the teacher while she was talking to someone's mother.

Katherine's own mother was waiting for her in the car outside the school.

"Hey, Mom," Katherine said as she slid into the back seat and slammed the door.

"Hello, Katherine." Her mother looked in the rearview mirror at her daughter as she eased the car out on to Bloor Street.

It was Friday night, and they were heading to the shopping mall to buy Katherine some new runners and jeans. She'd had a sudden growth spurt, and all the new fall clothes they had bought for her just last month were already too small.

"You're kind of late. Is everything okay?"

You're the second adult to ask me that today, thought Katherine. She said to her mom, "Yeah. I had to stay a little late because I lost my math book and was a bit scattered today. I didn't sleep too well last night."

"How come?"

"Well, because of the raccoon fight in the backyard,

of course. It was so loud, I couldn't sleep at all."

Katherine's mother was quiet for a minute.

"Raccoon fight? In the backyard? Oh…" Her mother's voice suddenly grew cold.

She paused a moment, then demanded, "Katherine, are you sure that's what it was? Did you actually see raccoons? Something dragged the garbage lids everywhere and broke the dwarf's nose right off… I'm not sure raccoons…" her voice trailed off. She turned quickly to look at her daughter, and her eyes left the road a second too long.

"Mom, look out!" Katherine yelled. Her mother veered to miss the car coming toward them.

"Mom—what's wrong?" she was worried now.

"Nothing," her mother snapped. "I just don't want to talk about the backyard right now. Let's not discuss it."

"Okay, okay. Sorry."

They didn't get a chance to discuss it again anyway, since at that moment they pulled into the mall parking lot and went shopping.

This is what they bought for Katherine:

1 new hooded sweatshirt, blue
2 new pairs of pants, one cord, one jean
1 new pair of running shoes, red with white stripes

It took forever to shop for Katherine. Everything had to be tried on and tried on again. Katherine knew her mother would have been just as happy to grab the first thing she saw that even remotely fit her then get out. But Katherine was more like her dad when it came to shopping. She had to find the right shoes, the right pants, the right sweatshirt. It took awhile.

That night at home, Katherine tried everything on again, then settled on her new cords and her cool red runners with the white stripes.

After dinner, she sat outside with Milly on the back porch for a little while to get used to her new clothes. Her mom and dad had their coffee out there too. It was a really warm night for mid-October, probably the last night of the year that they'd be able to sit outside together. It was really pretty, with the little Christmas lights running all around the back fence, and the moon-candles lit up here and there among the statues.

Flickering candlelight bounced off the deep chin of the cherub statue and made him look like he was laughing. The light made the unicorn look as though he was flashing his horn back and forth. The water falling from his horn into the pool around him made a gentle lapping sound.

It was very peaceful and serene.

Katherine took her new shoes off and felt the cooling grass between her toes. They chatted and her dad played some quiet guitar. When her parents went in, her mother said, "Five more minutes, Kath, then you come in too. Bring Milly in with you, I don't want her out all night." If Katherine didn't know better, she'd have said her mother gave the backyard a quick, dark look.

"Sure, Mom," she said and moved off the porch to the back of the yard to swing a little. Milly followed her.

She sat in the swing and listened to the sound of the city around her.

Someone was smoking a pipe nearby. Katherine

wrinkled up her nose at the hot, strange smell. Nobody around here smoked. It was probably someone visiting a neighbour in another small backyard one or two houses away, but she didn't like it.

A fire truck was screaming somewhere off in the distance. There was a police car too. The neighbour's dog was barking. Katherine had to concentrate to hear him. She was so used to the sound of him barking that she didn't really hear him any more. It was just background noise.

Suddenly something moved beside her. She jumped right off the swing onto her feet with her fists clenched.

Milly had disappeared into the bushes and came out growling.

"Milly, don't scare me like that!" Katherine said.

As she said it, she thought she heard another noise, very quiet but distinct. It was like a little chuckle.

Who would be laughing at her? Everything was quiet now. Even the neighbour's dog stopped barking.

"What the heck? What's going on in there?" Katherine, who was a brave twelve-year-old, didn't think twice about going into the bushes to check out the noise. She crept up to the bushes and quickly pulled them apart.

Her face broke into a smile. The gargoyle was sitting there.

"What are you doing in there?" she asked, surprised. "You shouldn't be in the bushes. I wonder why Mom put you in there?"

She reached in and picked up the little gargoyle,

heaving him high. She was expecting him to be much heavier than he was and was surprised when he weighed only a little more than Milly. Sometimes she helped her mom move the dwarves around, and they were much heavier than the gargoyle, although they were about his size.

Katherine noticed something else, too. The gargoyle was oddly warm. She wondered if he was made of something other than clay or stone.

"What are you made of, little gargoyle? Plastic or something?"

She placed him back on his pedestal beside the swing. Milly watched from a distance with disgust on her cat face, growling softly and twitching her tail.

"What is it, Mil? Don't you like Mr. Gargoyle? Hmmm?"

Katherine tried to catch Milly and take her over to see the gargoyle, but the cat was too quick for her and darted up the garden toward the house, spitting all the way.

Katherine laughed, patted the gargoyle's head and walked toward the house.

Milly never took her big cat eyes off the gargoyle, which is why she was the only one to see him stick his tongue out at Katherine's back as she walked away.

Cats are very wise, aren't they?

Chapter Four
Moonlight Dance

That night the backyard was much quieter. There were no raccoons fighting or banging garbage cans, no broken dwarves. It was just a still, cold night.

In fact, it was a little too cold. Suddenly the weather had turned chilly. It was definitely autumn.

The cold woke Katherine up on and off, but she didn't really mind. She liked dozing under her big blanket, toasty and warm while her nose got cold. It felt a little like sleeping outside in the tent when she and her parents went camping. They went to Algonquin Park every August, and sometimes the nights were really chilly that far north.

Around three a.m., Katherine woke to see Milly in her window, growling and twitching her tail again.

"Milly," she whispered, "shhhhh. I'm trying to sleep. Come here, kitty, come sleep under the warm covers." She lifted the covers invitingly.

Milly usually slept with her, but not tonight. She stayed put, all her attention trained on the backyard. She ignored Katherine.

"C'mere, Mil!" Katherine demanded, a little louder.

She was annoyed at being woken up now and wanted to get back to sleep. But Milly-the-statue-cat wouldn't budge.

Katherine sighed and got out of bed. She had to go to the bathroom anyway. She padded off down the hall, as quietly as she could so she wouldn't wake her parents.

On her way back, she stopped to scratch Milly's ear and casually looked outside.

"What's so interest..." Katherine stopped mid-word and stifled a small scream.

There, dancing among the statues in the cold moonlight, was the gargoyle!

Katherine was so dumbfounded that she slumped to the floor, her hand covering her mouth in shock. She shook her head back and forth in disbelief, barely breathing.

"No, it can't be," she said. "No way is there a gargoyle dancing around in my backyard. It's just a trick of the light or something." She looked around her familiar room for a moment to make sure she wasn't seeing things in there, too. Everything seemed pretty normal, no dancing teddy bears or walking furniture. She decided she wasn't completely losing her grip on reality.

She breathed deeply, drew up all her courage, and as quietly and bravely as she could, peeked over the bottom of the window into the backyard.

The gargoyle wasn't dancing any more. In fact, he was standing perfectly still. "That's better," she thought, "see, you were imagining it."

But she knew in her heart she hadn't imagined it. It made sense. It explained why he was so light and warm when she picked him up. It explained the chuckle she'd heard: he *was* laughing at her. It explained the "raccoon fight" the night before, and the dwarf's broken nose, and why Milly didn't like him.

It explained a lot of things.

As Katherine was putting the pieces in place, she didn't notice that the gargoyle had turned and was looking up at her window. He was looking directly at her.

BANG! She jumped as something hit the window right beside her head. The gargoyle had thrown a stone at her to get her attention.

"Hey!" she shouted and came back to her senses. She was looking straight into the backyard, straight into his glittering, dark eyes.

Chapter five
Ballerinas and Daisies

At this point, most twelve-year-olds would have gone for help. Or at the very least gone shrieking down the hall and jumped under the covers of their parents' bed.

Katherine did neither of these things. Instead, she stared the gargoyle right in the eye and tried to look fierce. Milly growled encouragement. Katherine gulped. She inched her window open a crack, and as quietly as she could, whisper-shouted down to the gargoyle.

"Hey! What the heck are you doing? You can't throw stones at my window!"

The gargoyle didn't miss a beat. He squared his little shoulders, stuck his tongue out at her, then smiled. His tiny lips pulled apart to show a very sharp row of glittering points. It was a sneering smile, not a cheerful, welcoming, happy smile.

She was a little offended and surprised at his rudeness. "You're really rude!" she yelled quietly. "Don't just smile at me. Explain yourself!" Katherine knew this last command was a rather weak one, copied from unimaginative adults trying to "get to the bottom of things", but it was all she could come up with at the moment.

Then she heard a low chuckle, the same chuckle she'd heard the night before in the bushes, and he stuck his tongue out at her once more, turning his back on her.

"How rude! He really *is* rude, Milly." Katherine was getting annoyed with him now. Who did he think he was? This was her house, her backyard, after all.

She and Milly could only watch helplessly as he walked casually over to the back door and bent down to pick something up. He knew he was being watched, but he didn't seem to care.

Have you ever seen a gargoyle walk? It isn't very pretty or graceful. It's really more of a waddle, since they have very thick legs, wide sharp-toed feet, and their arms drag along the ground. They tend to look somewhat off balance, since their leathery wings are very heavy and throw them backwards. It makes them look slightly "off-kilter", as Katherine's grandmother would say.

Katherine was wondering what he was picking up? He seemed very interested in his squat little feet and was doing something to them.

Suddenly, it came to her. Her shoes! She had left her new red shoes with the white stripes beside the back door!

"Oh, no!" she groaned. As he waddled back into full view, she realized to her dismay that she was right. The gargoyle had taken her shoes and stuffed them onto his own ugly feet!

Katherine was too astonished to do anything. She could only watch aghast at what happened next.

The gargoyle did a ridiculous pirouette, pointing one of his feet wearing her new shoe as high as he could toward the sky. Katherine would have found it funny if she wasn't so annoyed. Then he put his arms above his head and started prancing around, pretending to be a ballerina.

Katherine and her parents had seen the Canadian National Ballet perform *The Nutcracker* the Christmas before, so she knew what real ballerinas looked like. They were dainty and graceful.

The gargoyle's performance wasn't anything like that. He looked like an ungainly and ugly monster, aping something beautiful. It didn't seem to matter to him that he looked freakish and frightening. He tried all the moves anyway. The jumps, the spins, the positions, the leaps. All he needed was a frilly pink tutu around his waist.

Katherine shook her head and plucked up the nerve to speak to him out the window again.

"Hey, stupid gargoyle, take off my new shoes!" she yelled as loudly as she dared. She really didn't want to wake up her parents. Things were just getting interesting now that the initial shock of seeing the gargoyle alive in her backyard was beginning to wear off.

He stopped dead and turned to look up at her in mid-pirouette. "He really does look hysterical," she thought, "but I can't laugh now that he's looking at me." Despite herself, Katherine had a half-smile on her face.

Then the gargoyle spoke.

Have you ever heard a gargoyle speak? It's unlikely, I know, but they do speak. They sound like leaves rustling in winter, and although they don't speak English, or most of them don't, children can understand their language without any interpretation. It's a gift most children lose when they turn twelve or so (although some very wise children manage to keep the gift all their lives).

This is what he said: "Morgle mount flishin benjor taminki." This is what Katherine heard his whispery voice say: "Did you call me stupid, little girl?"

She was caught off guard, she was so surprised. What was going on? But she wasn't going to be silent and miss her chance to get her new shoes off his feet.

"Uh, yes," she stammered, "I guess I did." She grew defiant, and stuck her chin out. "Now take off my shoes!"

"Methol ment triagra." Which meant: "Hmm, no I think not. I like these shoes."

Then he proceeded to do the most awful thing that Katherine could think of. She watched, speechless with indignation and horror.

In her brand new shoes, he walked over to her mother's prize-winning New England Asters and started stomping on them. With big, athletic jumps, he hovered, then landed, again and again, until all the beautiful purple flowers lay trampled on the grass in a ruined pile.

"NO!" she shrieked. "No, stop! You're ruining my mother's asters! Stop it!" She wasn't being quiet any longer. All thought of her sleeping parents had long fled from her mind. She just wanted that awful monster to stop stomping her mother's beautiful prize-winning flowers IN HER SHOES.

But it was no use. It seemed to her that the more she yelled at him to stop, the harder he stomped, and the more he enjoyed it. He wore a sneering smile the entire time, giggling and chortling with glee.

And if you've never heard a gargoyle giggle and chortle with glee, it's just as well. It sounds like a bucket full of rusty nails being dropped onto the top of your parents' brand new car.

Chapter Six
Utterly Hopeless

You're probably wondering what happened next?

Well, Katherine didn't have many choices. And if you can think of a different way to handle the situation than any of these three choices below, then you're very wise and clever!

Choice #1. If you're a sensible sort of person, you're probably wondering if she got her parents out of bed and explained what happened.

Well, think about that for a minute. If you woke your parents out of a sound sleep and started talking nonsense about a gargoyle stomping the flowers in your new shoes, would they believe you? Or would they think you had stomped the flowers yourself and were trying to blame it on someone, or in this case *something* else?

So that was out.

Choice #2. If you're an adventurous and brave sort of person, you might be wondering if she ran downstairs and went outside to try to make the gargoyle stop?

This would seem like the most sensible thing to do, but Katherine found that she was suddenly a little afraid of facing the gargoyle in the middle of the dark, cold night all alone. Even if Milly did come to help her, Katherine didn't think she was quite brave enough for that.

So that was out.

Choice #3. Although this probably didn't occur to anyone, since it's so terribly dull, did she do nothing and go back to bed, convinced it was all just a VERY BAD DREAM? Sometimes a thing that seems the most unlikely is the very thing that actually happens.

So it was with Katherine after the gargoyle had stomped all her mother's flowers to bits.

She watched, helpless and sad, until he finally stopped, tired out from all the stomping. Then he flung her shoes off his feet and left them where they landed among the devastation.

After that, he simply waddled back to his little stone pedestal, hopped up and turned his back to her, apparently content to look like a statue once again.

Katherine was suddenly very tired and a little shaky from the cold. She didn't know what to do, so she did nothing. She closed her window and turned her back on it, then walked slowly back to bed and climbed under the covers, all the while with a very puzzled look on her face.

There was nothing else to do. She cried herself to sleep and slept fitfully until morning.

Chapter Seven
Decisions

Morning sun pierced through the bottom of the window blind deep into Katherine's room.

It was very cold, and she woke with a start, sitting bolt upright in bed. The events of the night before came flooding back to her.

She fell back onto the pillow and groaned. She couldn't begin to think what her parents were going to say when they noticed her shoes among the ruined flowers.

It was Saturday, so both of them were at home. She listened carefully and could hear them both moving around in the kitchen below her, getting breakfast ready, just like any ordinary Saturday morning.

They were letting her sleep in! She wasn't in trouble yet, which could mean only one thing: they hadn't noticed the damage.

She was wondering what she was going to say to them. What could she possibly say? The truth seemed like a big, ridiculous lie. And, in a completely confusing and unfair twist, a lie would sound so much more like the truth.

Katherine ran through a few possibilities:

"Mom, I was really mad that I had to stay after school, so I stomped your flowers."

No, that was no good.

"Mom, I really hate the dinner you made me last night, so I stomped your flowers."

No, that wouldn't work either.

"Mom, the gargoyle did it."

Hopeless. Utterly hopeless.

She was looking up at the light above her bed when a blood-curdling scream filled the house.

"OH MY GOSH! NOT MY FLOWERS! HANK, THE FLOWERS! LOOK AT THEM! THEY'RE RUINED!"

She heard the back door open, then slam. Then silence.

Without getting up to look out the window, she knew her parents were frantically running across the lawn to look at the damage. She also knew without looking that the gargoyle was sitting scrunched up on his pedestal, statue-like, watching the fun. Grinning, most likely.

Quite unexpectedly, Katherine felt a flash of hot anger flood her body. Why should that stupid gargoyle treat her family so badly? Why should he get away with it and make it look like she had done it?

Why? She suddenly knew what she had to do.

She got out of bed and slowly descended the stairs to the kitchen. She walked to the back door and silently opened it for her parents as they solemnly marched back into the house, too shocked to speak to her or to each other.

Neither of them was looking at her. Instead, they sat at the kitchen table and stared at their hands.

Katherine turned off the forgotten stove, where the pan was beginning to smoke, and turned to them.

"Mom, Dad," she began boldly, "I know what you're thinking. You're thinking I stomped all over your flowers in my new shoes."

She looked at them for encouragement. They were both looking at her now with nearly blank expressions. But at least they were listening. She pressed on.

"It looks bad, I know," she continued, "but I swear to you I didn't do it. I'm going to tell you the truth," she hesitated and bit her lip, "only it's going to sound kind of crazy."

At the word "crazy", her mother's head shot up and her mouth opened. She was looking hard at Katherine with a funny, dazed expression on her face. She was barely breathing.

"You know, you know..." Katherine trailed off.

What am I afraid of? she asked herself. *It's the truth. I have to tell it, I have to get them to believe me. They're my parents, after all. They will believe me, won't they?* She took a deep breath and started again.

"Mom, Dad, the gargoyle did it," she blurted out finally. She breathed out deeply and looked her parents in the eyes. It felt good to tell the truth, no matter how crazy it sounded.

Her parents did two different things at the same time. Her father burst out laughing. Her mother, however, groaned, then dropped her head into her hands and started crying.

Neither Katherine nor her dad was expecting that. They both rushed to her mother's side.

"What is it, Mom?" Katherine asked.

"What is it, Marie?" asked her dad, looking worried. They pulled up chairs and sat beside her, trying to comfort her.

She was muttering through her hands. "Not that stupid gargoyle! It can't be! Not again!"

Katherine's dad was clearly worried about his wife, but Katherine started to wonder what her mother knew. Or thought she knew.

She decided to try a new tack with her mother. She pressed a cup of tea into her mother's hands and put her hand gently on her shoulder.

"Mom," she said quietly, "where did you get that gargoyle? I mean, you seem to believe me that it was him, and I'm really glad you do, but you must know that he's..." she stopped. She couldn't bring herself to say it.

"Alive?" her mother said suddenly, snapping her head up to look Katherine in the face. "Yes! I know he's alive, Katherine..."

Katherine and her dad stared at her in silence. The room stayed perfectly quiet for what seemed like an eternity. Katherine could hear the kitchen clock above her mother's head ticking louder than ever before. The fridge motor buzzed around them like a car alarm.

Then her father finally spoke. "Marie," her father said gently, clearly making an effort to speak calmly. "Can you start at the beginning? Where did you get the gargoyle?"

Her mother had calmed down a bit in the long silence, having finally admitted to her family that she knew the gargoyle was a living creature. She blew her nose loudly, took a sip of tea, then started with her story.

"Okay, okay. I can't hide it any longer." She sighed. "It all started about a month ago, while I was walking to work at the agency office. You know I walk past The Golden Nautilus comic bookstore every day?" She looked at Katherine and her husband for encouragement.

They both nodded at her.

Katherine's dad said, "Go on, honey." It occurred to Katherine that this must sound really crazy to her poor dad, so she leaned in to him and let him know she loved him, too. Good old Dad. What must he think of his crazy daughter and wife?

"Well, one day I noticed there was this little gargoyle sitting in the window. I liked the look of him. He was kind of sweet looking. I dunno, just like he was thinking about something or looking off into the distance for someone. Anyway, I started to smile at him every day when I went by. Sounds crazy, I know, but you know I like statues..." Her mother smiled at them weakly, took a steadying sip of her tea and continued. "Some days I would wave at him, some days just smile. Then one day I said "Hi there" to him as I walked past, and he stuck his tongue out at me!" She started to get upset at this point, so Katherine's dad rubbed her shoulder and told her to go on.

"I know, Mom, he stuck his tongue out at me last

night, too. He's really rude!" said Katherine, helpfully. Again, her mother smiled at them and got a little braver. She went on with her story:

"I told myself that gargoyles DO stick their tongues out to drain water off rooftops. Gargoyles are drainspouts, at least they were ages ago. I thought he might have stuck his tongue out at me because he was really spouting water…"

"Spouting water, Mom? I haven't seen any water coming out of his mouth," Katherine said, unconvinced.

"No, I suppose I haven't either. But it could be a gargoyle reflex or something, sort of like sneezing? I didn't know what else to think… " Katherine's mother sighed. She took another sip of tea, and continued.

"Well, this went on for days. I'd look at the window, and there he'd be. I'd tell myself I was hallucinating, and it was just in my mind, so I'd keep walking. Just when I thought I'd imagined it, and it wasn't going to happen this time, he'd stick his tongue out at me again. Honestly, I thought I was going crazy! I'm so glad I'm not!" She turned to Katherine with a thankful look.

"Well, why did you buy him?" her father asked, a little bewildered. "I mean, if he was so rude and real and scary, why?" Her dad was floundering, clearly over his head at this point.

"Oh, I didn't buy him. I stole him."

Katherine and her dad both gasped.

"Mom! You *stole* him?" Katherine said, shocked.

"Well, actually, I guess I didn't really steal him. It's

kind of confusing. It was a nice day a few days ago, you know. And I was walking past the store again, but this time he was sitting outside on the sidewalk. So as I walked by, I tried to ignore him, but sure enough he stuck his tongue out at me again. Well, that was it. I kind of snapped, I guess. I didn't mean to, but I couldn't help it. My foot just went out and I gave him a little tap with my toe. I had to see if he was alive, or what he was..."

"You mean you kicked him?" her father asked bluntly.

"Well," she nodded sheepishly, "yeah. I guess I gave him a little kick. To see if he was real." The three of them giggled nervously.

Her mother went on quickly after that, wanting to get the story over with.

"And being the creature he is, he couldn't stand being kicked, so he started to follow me down the street, saying the most terrible things to me in his whispery voice! I tried to ignore him, I really did, but it was so weird having a gargoyle following me down the street talking to me, that suddenly I just reached back and grabbed him and stuffed him under my coat. I mean, I didn't want anyone to see me being followed by a gargoyle! Then I realized I was stealing him, so I ran as fast as I could all the way home."

"What did you do when you got home?" her dad asked.

"Well, I dropped him off in the backyard and have tried to ignore him ever since. I kind of hoped he would just go away."

"Well we have to get rid of him somehow, Mom. He's mean. And tricky. And kind of scary."

There was a long silence as the three of them thought about their situation. Just how, they were all wondering, do you get rid of a gargoyle?

Chapter Eight
Gargoth of Tallus

Over breakfast, they came up with a plan.

They decided that Katherine's mom probably shouldn't try to talk to the gargoyle. They felt it was best if Katherine talked to him, with her parents in the background standing guard.

They wanted Katherine to find out three things:
1. Why the gargoyle followed Katherine's mother home.
2. Why he wouldn't go away.
3. Why he was so rude and destructive.

After breakfast, and after several false starts, the three of them plucked up their courage and carefully opened the back door a crack, peering out into the yard. Katherine's dad had his fishing net over his shoulder, just in case. Milly peered out from between their legs.

There were the other statues, minus the broken dwarf who had been taken to the garden store to get his nose fixed.

But there was no gargoyle.

They stood on the back porch and looked carefully over the whole yard. He wasn't on his pedestal. He wasn't lurking among the remaining dwarves. He wasn't dancing in the flowers. He just wasn't there.

Then Katherine smelled a familiar odour. "Somebody is smoking a pipe again," she thought. "I wonder..." She made a "SHHH" sign at her parents.

She stepped gingerly off the back porch and tiptoed quietly across the backyard to the bushes beside the swing. She sniffed. Sure enough, there was the pipe smell again, only stronger this time. *Just like the other night*, Katherine thought. She looked back at her parents, then pointed to the bushes.

"He's in there!" she mouthed silently. She hoped they understood her. They both nodded, and looked worried.

"Be careful!" her mother mouthed back.

Katherine took a deep breath then approached the bushes. She was just about to part them, when a whispery voice said, "Gargol snarthen felamont."

Katherine heard the voice say, "I wouldn't do that if I were you, little girl."

Katherine jumped back. Her mother gasped.

As she and her parents watched, the bushes parted and out stepped the gargoyle.

He had a small pipe stuck between his teeth and looked just like a fine gentleman out for a morning stroll, with a great inheritance and all the time in the world to enjoy it.

"Frahot bello northen gamet." Katherine and her mother heard, "Hello, to you all. You've found me!"

He stood by the bushes, his wings folded tightly behind him, and tapped his pipe out on the bottom of his scaly foot. Then he opened the little pouch at his side and placed his pipe carefully inside.

"Well, that explains the tobacco smell and the pouch," thought Katherine, pleased with herself for a moment.

The gargoyle took them all in for what seemed a very long time. Then he spoke again in his strange and wavery language: "I suppose you'd like me to introduce myself?"

Katherine and her mother nodded slowly at him. Katherine's dad just stared.

"Very well," he continued in gargoyle. "My name is Gargoth of Tallus. You may call me Gargoth. I'm just over four hundred years old, which is rather young for a gargoyle, and I'm afraid I've lost my way. I've been on a very long and dangerous journey, which, temporarily I hope, has stranded me in your ridiculous backyard."

At this point, the gargoyle waved his hand to take in the backyard and sighed deeply. He trudged slowly past Katherine and hopped up onto his pedestal beside the swing, every inch of him now looking dejected and sad.

Katherine had said nothing and felt at this point that she should speak back to him. She cast a backward glance at her mom and dad, who hadn't moved from the porch, then spoke.

She had an odd feeling that it was important to be as polite and grandiose as possible when addressing a gargoyle this close up, so she spoke like this: "Oh Gargoth of Tallus, I am Katherine, and this is my mother Marie and my father Hank. We are the Newberrys. We are sad to hear you are now stranded in our backyard among the other mythical creatures. To speak honestly, we are confused by your presence here as well. Why have you chosen to follow my mother? And why have you not left our backyard?"

She thought she might leave out the question about being so rude for a bit. Now that she was so close to him, knowing he was alive and not just a lump of plaster, she was remembering the sharp, shiny teeth from his smile in the moonlight the night before. She was fighting the rise of the unpleasant memory of being bitten by a small dog when she was a little girl. It was all too easy to imagine Gargoth's sharp little teeth snapping at her in anger.

She gulped and was going to continue, when her father spoke up in a quavery voice.

"Uhhh, what's that noise he's making?" he asked. He looked kind of pale and watery-eyed.

"Shhh, he's talking, Hank. Can't you hear him?" her mother said.

"Talking? You call that noise talking? It's more like sandpaper running over the inside of my head. It's just gibberish."

"You mean you can't understand him?" Katherine asked, suddenly a little panicky. "Mom, you can understand him, right?"

"Yes, yes, I can understand him just fine." Her mother looked confused.

"Allow me to explain," Gargoth broke in. "Only clever children and very special adults, indeed only one or two that I know of," at this he shot Katherine's mother a significant look, "can understand the ancient and sacred tongue of my race. Which is an answer to your first question: why did I follow your mother home? Because she could hear me. Because she could see me. And because she expected nothing from me in return."

At this, Gargoth cast his dark eyes to the grass and didn't look up again for a long while.

Katherine shot a glance at her mother, who was clearly very relieved to hear this explanation, such as it was. But Katherine thought she'd better do a little translating for her father, who looked completely lost.

"Uh, Dad, he says you can't understand him because only a very few adults can." She looked at her mother for help.

"Yes, Hank, it seems for some peculiar reason I can understand him, and you can't. He says children can hear gargoyles and understand them, but most adults, well, almost all adults I guess, can't for some reason. Except for me. I love statues...maybe that's it?" she finished, looking kind of lost herself. But still very relieved.

"Well, okay then. What's he doing here?" her father asked, determined to go on.

"He said Mom is the first adult to talk to him in a long time. I guess he's lonely? And when Mom could hear him and understand him, he followed her home. Is that it, Gargoth?" Katherine asked.

"His name is Gargoth?" her dad whispered.

"Yes, Hank, shush!" her mother said, nudging her husband to be quiet, because Gargoth was speaking again.

"You are right, Katherine," Gargoth said, his whispery

37

voice even sadder. He pronounced her name KAY-
THAR-EEN. "There have been a few who can see me,
who have spoken to me, but most often they were my
enemies." As he said these last words, Gargoth's voice
grew bitter.

"Your mother is different. She spoke to me and
addressed me without fear. I have been terribly alone.
I hoped she could help."

Thinking of their second question, Katherine
started in: "Well, isn't there someone else who could
help you? I mean," she corrected herself quickly, "oh
Gargoth, is there not another who could help you find
your way again?"

Gargoth smiled at this. For the first time, a genuine
smile. "Don't worry, human child, I am not offended.
I know that you do not wish me here. I know that in
your world, I am but a plaything or an object of curiosity,
long forgotten and misplaced. Captured on the roofs of
buildings or churches for amusement or to spout water
into dark alleys. Stuck in backyards among the dwarves."

He paused a long time and turned to look at Milly,
who had joined the family on the back porch, sitting at
her owners' feet. She kept her distance.

"No, sadly Katherine, there is no other who can help
me. I have waited. I have watched. Your mother spoke
to me without greed or malice in her heart, and so I
believe only she can help me find my way again."

Katherine was thinking hard. "Do you mean,
because Mom said "Hi there" to you that day on the
street, that you are somehow connected to her? Like a
servant, or something?"

At the word "servant", Gargoth flinched and hunched his little shoulders even more deeply. A dark frown was upon his face. "No, not a servant as you know it. But I am indebted to her in a way you may not ever understand. She saw me. She spoke to me. I am hers until I find my way again."

With that, Gargoth turned his head away and would speak no further despite Katherine's attempt to continue their conversation.

Katherine's mother walked slowly across the yard. She stopped in front of the little gargoyle, who had his back to her, and reached out to him. Gently she stroked Gargoth's leathery wings with one hand. Gargoth turned his face to her.

Hot gargoyle tears were streaming down his cheeks and splashing with a "hiss" onto the cold stone pedestal beneath his feet.

Chapter Nine
House Guest

After that, Katherine and her parents left Gargoth alone for the rest of the day. He seemed content to sit on his pedestal and stare gloomily at the tree.

Katherine and her mother spent most of the rest of the morning sitting at the kitchen table, trying to explain to Katherine's father what the gargoyle had said.

As far as they could figure out, they explained, Katherine's mother had been the first adult to speak "without malice" to Gargoth in ages, maybe hundreds of years.

This made Gargoth want to speak to her. This also somehow made him "hers", but not in a servant-like way. Her father wanted to know everything that was said at this point, particularly about being "hers", but this had them as lost as he was.

Clearly Gargoth was very sad and had talked about being "lost", but in this first conversation they didn't really have the chance to clear that up. How was he lost? Who had lost him? Were there other gargoyles like him somewhere in the world? Was there any way to help him? He didn't seem to think anyone could help but Katherine's mother.

And he didn't seem very interested in going away.

On the plus side, he hadn't stuck his tongue out at them since they had started talking to him, so maybe they had won a very slight victory on that count. Katherine's mother still thought the gargoyle stuck his tongue out as a kind of downspout reflex, but Katherine wasn't totally convinced; she thought he was just being rude.

Rude or not, they decided that he was going to have to stay in the backyard until Monday, then they would make a clear plan about what to do with him.

Katherine caught her mother stealing glances out the back window at the gargoyle all day. Finally, at dinner time, her mother went out to the backyard alone and talked once more to Gargoth, then returned and started putting apples into a basket.

"What are you doing, Mom?" Katherine asked.

"He's hungry," she said simply, and with that emptied the fridge of all the apples they owned and slipped back outside.

She didn't come back in for a long time.

Chapter Ten
The Golden Nautilus

Katherine and her parents spent that weekend trying hard to act as though nothing odd or unusual was going on. They had decided not to mention Gargoth again until Monday, so the rest of the weekend came and went as normally as possible, considering the events of Saturday morning. Katherine found she didn't even want to look out the back window, and she and her parents were really, really polite with each other.

Her dad was quiet all weekend, but her mother seemed unnaturally chatty and perky, doing the talking for all three of them at every meal. She got like that when she was especially nervous about something.

Milly didn't want to go out the back door.

Oddly, Katherine found she didn't want to leave the house either. When her friend Rubie invited her over on Saturday night for a sleepover, she didn't want to go anywhere. She made up an excuse and stayed in.

The only tricky bit of the weekend came on Sunday night. The family was invited to the neighbours' house for Sunday night dinner, and her mom and dad couldn't think of a good enough reason to say "no" on such short notice.

The McDonalds were probably the best neighbours anyone ever had, anywhere, in the history of neighbourly kindness. They were quite a bit older than Katherine's parents, and they had no children of their own, so Katherine was always terribly spoiled when she went to their house. Mr. McDonald always gave her a special treat, and often Mrs. McDonald had rented a new movie or game for her to play while the adults were talking over dinner. It was always a highlight of the week for Katherine. They had babysat her often when she was little. She got to stay up late, snuggled warmly on the couch between these two fine people, and watch late night TV, which was strictly forbidden when her parents were home.

They were the kind of neighbours who watched the house when Katherine and her parents went away on holiday. The kind of neighbours who took Milly into their home on short notice. They were, in fact, the kind of neighbours you could call on any time of the day or night, and they'd be happy to help.

They were her second family.

But for the first time in her life, Katherine found herself being shy when Mr. McDonald asked if the asters were still in bloom.

Later, when Mrs. McDonald asked if she could come and see the flowers because she liked them best in their final blaze of glory, both of Katherine's parents yelled, "No! It's not a good time right now." Then they had to apologize and explain they were just a little on edge because it hadn't been a good growing season for them, and they had been hoping to win another "Small Garden" award this year.

Katherine caught her dad mopping his brow with a napkin after that little lie.

They left early, as their good neighbours stood bewildered in their doorway, waving goodbye.

For his part, Gargoth had stayed motionless on his pedestal almost the entire weekend, occasionally discarding apple cores, which slowly piled up around his feet.

Finally, Monday came, and the family was able to get back to some degree of normal life. At breakfast, Katherine's mother said she was going to visit The Golden Nautilus after work and see if she could find out anything about Gargoth, such as where he came from. It was the first time in two days that any of them had mentioned him.

"And Katherine, I want you to come. When I get you from school, we'll go straight there."

Katherine's dad shot her an "I'm sorry" look, then bolted for work, clearly glad to be out of the world of gargoyles and back into the world of science and students. This was likely because there was little risk of anything inanimate coming to life in the safe, predictable world of his classroom (with the possible exception of some senior students at the back of the room who hadn't said a word all term).

It was possibly Katherine's longest day in school ever. It seemed like it would never end. In history class, the last period of the day, Mrs. Glean droned on so long about the prairies and pioneer life, that Katherine decided it must have been the most boring time in Canadian history. She jumped when the boy sitting next to her hit his head on the desk with a loud "thud". Asleep.

After what seemed like years, the three-thirty bell rang and Katherine dashed for the door, but unfortunately not before Mrs. Glean could corner her, once again wearing a worried expression.

"Katherine," she smiled nicely, "you're still not concentrating very well. Are you able to see the board okay, dear?"

Great, thought Katherine, *now my teacher thinks I'm blind.*

"Oh, yes, everything is just fine, really Mrs. Glean. We did a lot of...um, gardening this weekend, and I'm a little tired. You know, with my parents' award-winning flowers and everything..." Katherine feigned a smile then dashed past the teacher before she could say anything else. She hoped this rather lame excuse would satisfy her teacher for now. She was getting awfully snoopy.

"How persistent can you be?" Katherine wondered as she trudged out into the street, looking for her mother's car. She frowned. Her mother wasn't there. She stood in the cold for a few minutes, biting her lip.

Suddenly her mother's car appeared from around the corner, lurching and careening down the street toward her. The car looked out of control. Students ran for cover, screaming. The car slammed to a stop in front of Katherine, then the back door burst open. Her mother leaned into the back seat from the front, and yelled at her, "GET IN!"

Katherine was too shocked to do anything but obey.

She jumped into the car, and they sped off. She noticed her mother's hair was loose and messy, jumbled all over her face, and she was breathing in a funny, jagged way. She looked flustered and a little crazy. Katherine was worried.

"Mom, what's wrong..." Katherine started, then stopped. That was when she noticed the large cloth bag in the seat beside her. It wiggled slightly.

Katherine clasped her hand to her mouth. "MOM! You didn't bring *him?!*" she shouted. But she knew the answer. Her heart sank. What was her mother doing, bringing the gargoyle in the car *to school?* At that moment, Gargoth popped his head out of the bag and glared at her.

She tried not to look too horrified. She even managed a weak smile at Gargoth. He stuck his tongue out at her and dived back into the bag. *So much for no more rudeness,* she thought.

"Mom, what's going on?" she asked. "Why did you bring him? This can't be a wise thing to do. Mom?"

Her mother was staring at the traffic, apparently not listening.

"Mom," she started again, "why is your hair all messy?"

"Gargoth has never been inside a car before," she said simply. That was all the explanation Katherine was going to get. They drove in silence until her mother pulled the car into a parking spot in front of The Golden Nautilus.

"Bring him," her mother said to her as she got out of the car, attempting to fix her mussed hair. Katherine could see it was useless to argue, since her mother was already clopping unsteadily across the sidewalk toward the store. Katherine looked toward the bag, then moved closer and peered in.

Gargoth was huddled, cowering and shivering, in the bottom of the bag. Clearly, he was very frightened. Katherine suddenly felt a tiny bolt of sympathy for him. He glared at her, then shut his eyes, just like she had seen Milly do once when she had hurt her tail and was going to the vet.

"It's okay, Gargoth. We're just going to look in the store. Nothing will happen to you," she found herself saying gently.

He looked up at her again, then closed his eyes once more and stopped shivering. He drew his wings tightly around himself and sat still as a statue in the bottom of the bag.

Katherine picked up the bag and left the car. She entered the store behind her mother. It was a dark dungeon of a store, full of strange and delightful things. Books, comics, unusual toys and strange knick-knacks, candles, skulls and superheroes. There were dragons, monsters and other magical creatures. She and her mother nosed around the shelves but could find nothing resembling a gargoyle.

"May I help you?" A young salesman finally appeared, looking bored.

"Yes, yes, we're looking for a gargoyle? Do you have any?" Katherine's mother asked.

The young man was looking at her mother closely. "No, no, we don't," he said. "We had one last week, but it disappeared." Katherine's mother started to look uncomfortable. "But hold on, I'll check if there are any new gargoyles in stock in the back." He left them for what seemed like ages.

When he returned, he was carrying a gargoyle. It was the perfect twin of Gargoth. He placed it on the shelf in front of them.

"We just got this one in, but that's it. The supplier doesn't make them any more," he panted. The store room must have been a long way off.

"Thank you," her mother said. "Where did you order them from?" she asked as nonchalantly as possible.

"This one came from New York somewhere," he said, then walked away to help another customer.

When they were alone, Katherine's mother bent down and whispered to Gargoth. "There's another gargoyle here, he looks just like you. Look..."

She held the bag up close to the shelf, and Gargoth popped his head out, face to face with the little gargoyle. In an instant, he was out of the bag, with his hands clasped tightly around the statue's neck, snarling and snapping his teeth together like a possessed demon. Then things really got interesting.

Chapter Eleven
Near Escape

Several things happened at once.

Katherine's mother was quicker than Gargoth, and she grabbed him, but only managed to grab him by a wing. This made him angry, and he snatched up his statue twin and started to swing it over his head at her.

Katherine was trying desperately to get the bag back over Gargoth's head, but with his wing spread out and swinging the other statue with all his might, he was too big and cumbersome to fit.

A teenager wearing a black T-shirt and black lipstick had been watching Katherine and her mother over the nearest comic book rack. Now she was running back toward the counter and the young salesman yelling, "Hey! Come see this!" at the top of her lungs.

A second later, Katherine and her mother saw the store owner running towards them, waving a broom.

"What's he going to do with *that?*" Katherine wondered. Before she knew what was happening, her mother grabbed her, the bag, and the struggling gargoyle, who was still clutching the statue, and was pushing them towards the door.

"Drop it! Please, Gargoth, drop the statue!" her mother was pleading, as they ran down the sidewalk, Katherine in the rear. Katherine looked behind her for a moment, then back at her mother just in time to see the gargoyle statue fly into the air—Gargoth had thrown it in his rage. Katherine rushed forward to catch the statue and was nearly knocked over by its weight. She placed it gingerly on the sidewalk before tearing off after her mother.

As they sped off in the car down Queen Street, Katherine saw several employees burst out of the store, with the owner at the head, still brandishing his broom. The young salesman bent to pick up the statue that Katherine had caught and placed, unharmed, on the sidewalk.

"At least we didn't steal anything," her mother gasped, breathless, her eyes on the road. "So we didn't do anything wrong..."

Katherine sank back into her seat, taking time to breathe. Then she looked over at the bag, now containing Gargoth. It was shaking. Expecting him to be cowering and frightened, she looked in the top to say something calming.

There in the bottom of the bag was a strange sight. Gargoth of Tallus was laughing.

And if you've ever seen a gargoyle laugh, you know it's not a pretty sight.

Chapter Twelve
The Flightless Bird

That night at dinner, Katherine's mother was trying to explain to her father what had happened at The Golden Nautilus that afternoon.

"He GRABBED the other statue?" he was asking in disbelief. "Marie, why did you take him there? What was the point?"

"I was hoping that he would see the other gargoyle and want to stay, that's all. I mean, if it had been alive, he would have wanted to stay, wouldn't he? I don't know...or maybe we could have found out where he was from, then return him there. It didn't seem like a bad idea at first..." She trailed off, upset.

Her father sighed, then leaned over and spoke gently to his wife. "It's okay, I guess. Clearly, they aren't going to arrest you for anything, and at least we know a few things now."

"What?" asked Katherine, looking up from her pasta.

"Well, we know that Gargoth is the only real gargoyle at The Golden Nautilus, that he was made in New York, and that the supplier isn't making them any more."

"If he is alive, there must be other gargoyles that are

alive, don't you think?" Katherine asked. "Maybe there are some others like him in other stores in Toronto. It might be worth trying to visit some of them to see."

"I'll look on the Internet to see if I can find out who supplied them to Canada," her mother said.

For his part, Gargoth wasn't very helpful. After they'd arrived home from The Golden Nautilus, Katherine's mother spent a full hour trying to get more information out of him. She sat in the backyard on a lawn chair beside his pedestal and questioned him about everything that had happened to him.

He was sulky from his misadventure and still frightened. Unfortunately, he wasn't very helpful and tended to talk in riddles, and even outright lies. Finally Katherine's mother gave up and left him with a fresh bag of apples to keep him company.

"I don't know what to do with him. One thing's for sure," she said with a smile at Katherine, "no more car trips, and no more trips to The Golden Nautilus."

"Mom, why was he so mad at the other statue?" Katherine asked.

Her mother looked sadly at her. "It's hard to say exactly. It seems that someone stole his image somehow, without his permission. I think he finds it terribly insulting to see himself recreated in a statue. He says he was kept against his will in an awful place for a long time."

"Couldn't he fly away?" Katherine asked, surprised.

"Oh, he can't fly!" her mother said.

"He can't? How come?" Katherine asked.

"I guess he never learned," her mother said mildly

and went back to her dinner.

Throughout the evening, Katherine found herself wandering to the back window to check on Gargoth, who was pacing sulkily back and forth among the dwarves.

Chapter Thirteen
Gargoth's Request

The rest of the week went by quietly with no further adventures.

Gargoth lived peacefully enough in their backyard, eating bags of apples and dropping the cores here and there among the statues. Once or twice Katherine caught him lobbing apple cores, using the mended dwarf for target practice, but her mother scolded him, and he sheepishly promised he wouldn't do it again.

In fact, he promised to be still and quiet during the days, and only move around at night, so the neighbours wouldn't become suspicious of him. Indeed, he was as good as gold, and as still as a statue most of the time.

He seemed content just to be himself, known finally to the family as a living, breathing thing. He was no longer so rude and surly, although if you caught him napping, he was apt to snap at you if you disturbed him.

After the near disaster at The Golden Nautilus, Katherine's parents decided it would be best to leave Gargoth in the backyard, where he couldn't cause any more trouble. This meant that any research they were going to do to track down his origins would be done from the comfort and safety of their computer, on the Internet. After a few short days, it began to seem almost normal to have a gargoyle living among the dwarves in their yard.

Even Milly asked to be let out at the back door, although she still refused to go anywhere near the gargoyle.

Katherine only talked to him once during that first week. She went back to his pedestal one chilly night after dinner, wearing her warmest coat, and took up a place on the swing. The leaves were falling from the tree now, and the evening was chilly enough for snow. Halloween was in one week.

"Gargoth," she started, "have you ever tried to fly?"

He looked at her mournfully. "Perhaps. A long time ago."

"But…did you learn?"

He sighed deeply. "No, Katherine. It can take a lifetime to learn to fly, and only another gargoyle can teach me. Otherwise I am doomed to fail."

Katherine thought about this for a moment. "Why does it have to be another gargoyle?" she asked.

Another sigh from Gargoth. "Because you must be taught by another who…" he hesitated, "who cares for you." He sunk his head into his leathery claws. "And I have no one."

He cast his eyes up to the sky. "It will snow soon, Katherine. I will be covered with a chilly winter blanket tonight."

For the first time it occurred to Katherine that he

might be uncomfortable living outside, especially now that the cold weather was coming.

"Gargoth, do you feel the cold? When it snows, I mean, will you be chilly?" she asked.

"Chilly? No, Katherine. I feel neither heat nor cold, only hunger and thirst, and your kind mother has seen that I do not suffer there." He waved toward a bag nearby, bursting with apples and a full jug of water.

They were quiet for a while, listening to the sounds of the city. Gargoth stirred on his pedestal, then he spoke again. "There is one thing I would like, though." He looked almost shyly at her, his heavy eyelids drooping slightly.

"Yes?"

"I would like to visit more gargoyles, in more stores in this city." He glanced at her sideways with a tiny curl of his lip.

She hesitated. "But you know my mom and dad want you to stay here, in the backyard. You're not supposed to go anywhere."

He didn't seem to hear her. "You know how to use the underground locomotion machine? Don't you?" Katherine thought for a moment and realized he must mean the subway.

"Yes, I do," she answered.

"Then, you can take me," he said slyly.

"Oh sure, Gargoth! You want me to smuggle you onto the subway and travel around the city with you looking at gargoyles. I really don't think so! Not after the way you acted at The Golden Nautilus! I don't want to get arrested!"

"I promise to behave," he said quietly, "and a gargoyle never breaks a promise."

"No way," she said simply.

There was a long pause, then Gargoth spoke again. "I would not ask you to do this for me, Katherine, but I believe there may be one among the gargoyles in a certain store in this city who can teach me to fly. We may be able to find her."

With the word "her", Katherine jumped off the swing and walked toward Gargoth. "What do you mean, 'her'?" she asked him. He turned his face away and would not answer.

She tried again. "What do you mean, Gargoth? Is there another gargoyle like you in Toronto? Do you know her? Where do you think she is? Tell me!" she insisted, impatient now.

Gargoth spoke quietly. "You do not need to shout, Katherine. I am unsure how much to tell you. I did not tell your mother, because I know she will not take me to find her. But I am telling you because you are a child, and you still think and believe like a child. You may be able to help me. But we will have to do it together, alone."

Katherine was just about to answer when her father opened the back door and called her in for bed.

"Coming, Dad," she yelled. She turned back to Gargoth, who reached out and took her hand. It was the first time he had touched her. His claw was leathery and cool. "Please think about it, Katherine," he said in his gargoyle voice, then dropped her hand and looked away.

"Okay, I'll think about it," she said then walked slowly back to the house.

What else could she say?

Chapter Fourteen
Hallowe'en

Halloween fell on a Saturday, and the day dawned cool and sunny.

It was a glorious day for carving pumpkins and getting the house ready for trick-or-treaters. Katherine had arranged to go trick-or-treating with her best friend Sarah, who lived just down the street, and Sarah's little brother Benjamin.

Katherine and her parents spent the day decorating the front yard and front porch of the house. Their usual trick was to fill a garbage bag with leaves and poke a single jean leg stuffed with newspapers and an old work boot out of the bottom of the bag. They also hung a skeleton from the front tree and swathed the house in fake spider webs. Every year, Katherine's dad said it was the last time they were going to use the awful sticky stuff because it was almost impossible to get rid of, but every year they used it anyway. Shreds of fluffy web puffed from every corner of the house all year long, as a constant reminder of Halloweens past.

At lunch time, Katherine looked into the backyard and noticed Gargoth looking very agitated. He was pacing quickly (as quickly as a short-legged gargoyle can) back and forth between his pedestal and the maple tree, all the while looking up into the sky. When he reached the tree, he looked quickly behind him, then started back to his pedestal. After she'd finished her soup and sandwich, Katherine went out to talk to him.

"What's the matter, Gargoth?" she asked.

He stopped his pacing and slumped to the grass. He looked very worried.

"Katherine, I feel that something terrible is going to happen."

"Why?"

"Because there are strange smells and noises in the air. There are strange creatures flying above me and stranger creatures still wandering by on the street."

At that moment, a noisy flock of Canada geese flew low overhead, heading for a landing in Lake Ontario to the south. It was not the first flock that had passed overhead that day, since the geese were beginning to migrate south for the winter in the last days of fall.

Gargoth dove into the bushes beside his pedestal, quaking with fear. Katherine parted the bushes and pulled him gently to standing.

"Gargoth, get a hold of yourself. They're just geese. See?" she said, pointing up as the familiar V-shape disappeared south of them. He refused to look up but continued staring steadfastly at the ground.

She decided to continue gently. "What else did you see that scared you?" she asked.

Gargoth looked up at her, clearly struggling with a

great fear welling up inside him.

He finally spoke and said, "There were strange beings with long black hair and ugly, frightening faces marching down the street. One carried a broom stick and the other a dead black cat."

Katherine laughed. "Gargoth, they were dressed up! It's Halloween! They were dressed like witches or something. Haven't you ever seen people dressed up for Halloween before?"

"No," he said simply. He was suddenly indignant with her because she had laughed at him.

"Where have you been? Halloween happens every October 31, and it's a festival of the dead. Don't tell me you've never seen it or heard of it before?"

Gargoth looked extremely hurt. "No, I have not seen it or heard of it before. It sounds terrifying. Why do people dress up like creatures of the dead?"

Katherine thought for a moment. He really seemed frightened by what he had seen.

"I'm sorry, Gargoth," she apologized. "I guess I'd be scared too. But you don't need to be. It's just for fun. People dress up in funny clothes like clowns, or scary clothes like monsters and witches and things. Then they go around the neighbourhood and collect candy from everyone, or they do something bad if you don't give them candy. Got it?"

At this point, Gargoth's eyes were as huge as half-moons, his face a mask of pure disbelief.

"Surely, Katherine," he said in his most dignified voice, "you do not expect me to believe such a childish, made-up story? In my past, when humans appeared in masks, it was usually the beginning of a terrible night of death. Almost always, someone was..." Here Gargoth stopped, apparently struggling with his memory, deciding whether or not to tell Katherine what was in his mind. He had no desire to frighten her.

He started again, more gently, "Katherine, do not forget that I have lived more than four hundred years. There was a time in my country when women who looked like those women I saw just now..."

"You mean the witches?" Katherine asked.

Gargoth nodded solemnly and took a deep breath to continue. "Yes, when women looked like that, they would be hunted and," here he dropped his voice to a whisper so Katherine had to move her head very close to his, "burned at the stake!"

Katherine stared at Gargoth. Her smile slowly died, as it occurred to her for the first time that Gargoth's experience of the world was very old indeed. And some of the things he must have seen were really scary and awful.

"Do you mean you saw witches burned at the stake?" she barely whispered.

Gargoth nodded again, his dark eyes solemn and very sad. "I saw more death than I cared to, Katherine. And the poor souls often looked like your Halloween witches..."

Despite his best efforts not to, Gargoth was remembering a terrible night in England, during the Burning Time. Black smoke and shouts of "Witch! Witch!" filled the air as he hid behind a church parapet, looking down into the burning field below him. *No*, thought Gargoth. *I cannot tell Katherine what I have seen.*

Gargoth took a deep breath, cleared his mind and looked up at Katherine. He managed a weak half-smile. "It was truly terrible, Katherine. An awful, sad time when people turned against their neighbours and could accuse them and have them killed as witches with no reason, no proof. If a man said a woman was a witch, she was tried and very likely killed."

They sat silently for some time. Katherine thought Gargoth's world must have been very ugly, dangerous and dark for much of his life. She also realized that he didn't know very much about her world at all.

She finally spoke. "There's nothing to fear, Gargoth. We don't burn people at the stake any more. I don't think we ever did that in Canada. Here people are put in prison if they do something really bad. They can even get out of prison later on. I'm sorry you saw something awful and frightening like that. You're safe here. Just stay in the backyard and you'll be fine. I'll tell Mom to come back to talk to you, okay?" She smiled what she hoped would be a reassuring smile and turned away.

She went back into the house to get ready for her night out with Sarah and Benjamin. For a while she couldn't help feeling sad that Gargoth had been so frightened and upset by what he had seen. But Halloween was Halloween, and in the excitement she eventually forgot about the gargoyle and his fear. But it might have been better for everyone if she had remembered to mention to her mother that Gargoth was worried about witches and didn't really know what Halloween was all about.

Around dinner time, Katherine's mother walked her down to Sarah's house and went over the rules with her.

"I know, Mom! No going into a house, no splitting up from Sarah and Benjamin, no eating anything until I bring it back and you check it out. I'll be careful! 'Bye!" And with that, she sprinted up to Sarah's door, waved to her mother, and vanished inside Sarah's house.

Katherine's mom walked slowly back down the street. As she glanced toward her own home, she thought she caught something out of the corner of her eye, vanishing around the side of her house.

"Must be Milly," she thought and forgot about it. But she probably shouldn't have.

Katherine and Sarah had decided to dress like rock stars, and Benjamin was going as a ghost. Around seven o'clock, Sarah's mom couldn't hold them back any longer and released the three kids to the street. They rushed down to the sidewalk, barely waving goodbye over their shoulders.

Their neighbourhood, being downtown with lots of houses and people, was the place to be! Almost every house had a pumpkin, and the candy was the best you could get. Chocolate bars, twizzlers, fat lollipops, chip bags, gum. No creepy caramels or cheap rockets in this neighbourhood!

The threesome set off down the street, jostling among the crowds of happy trick-or-treaters, grabbing their soon-to-be-bulging sacks at their sides.

Everything was ready to go at Katherine's house.

Her mom and dad always set up lawn chairs on the front porch, turned on creepy music inside the house, and opened the front window so it would lure trick-or-treaters up their street.

You should probably know that her parents also dressed up and sat perfectly still in the lawn chairs until kids came up the porch stairs. They usually waited until someone was reaching into the candy bowl on the table in front of them before they spoke, which of course usually got a scream or at the very least, a jump.

In fact, most kids in the neighbourhood grew up knowing that the Newberrys were sitting together behind the candy bowl and that the scarecrows or witches, or whatever was sitting there, were really them ready to pounce. Indeed, for most kids, it just wouldn't be Halloween without the Newberrys giving them a good scare.

This year her parents had dressed as witches. They were pretty convincing, too. And they were also very good at sitting completely still, looking like statues.

The first children were beginning to come up the street, and the littlest ones, the bunnies and bees and adorable three-year-old clowns, were always first. Katherine's parents stood up to welcome the first of the youngest kids (not wanting to scare anyone so young). A young dad, mom and baby angel were just starting up their walkway with happy, expectant looks when the baby screamed. The parents looked horrified and rushed past their house, shooting angry backward glances at Katherine's parents.

"What did we do, Hank?" her mother asked her dad.

"I don't know. Maybe we're just too scary this year?" he answered. "Let's tone it down a little."

So they decided that for the littlest kids, they would take off their scary witch masks. They sat without their ghoulish faces, smiling and waving at their neighbours, encouraging everyone to come and take some candy.

But it made no difference. Even with them sitting there, plainly not witches or scary people, not one single child would come to their door. In fact, quite the opposite. People would begin walking up their path then suddenly screech to a halt and bolt back on to the sidewalk, to disappear back up the street.

Katherine's parents were at a loss.

"I don't get it. What's wrong Marie?" Hank Newberry finally asked his wife.

"I don't know. We turned off the scary music. We got rid of the scary costumes. We look normal enough, don't we?" his wife answered.

With that, Katherine's dad walked off the porch and headed down to the street to look at his house from the sidewalk. "Maybe it's the skeleton," he was saying as he turned to look at his house from the street. But then he stopped dead in his tracks.

It wasn't the skeleton. It was Gargoth.

He was perched on the roof of the porch like a small eagle, squatting right above the lawn chairs where Katherine's parents were sitting, and out of their sight, but he was plain enough to those on the sidewalk. When he saw Katherine's dad, he spread his wings and flapped them lightly like a large, black bird might to straighten its feathers.

Hank's jaw fell open. He looked quickly up and down the street. Luckily it was empty for the moment.

"Gargoth! What are you doing up there? Get down!" he yelled.

Marie rushed off the porch to stand on the sidewalk beside her husband. She covered her gasp with her hand. Then she said as calmly as she could, "Gargoth, you are supposed to stay in the backyard, remember? It's really not okay for you to be frightening our neighbours like this. Please come down."

Sulkily, Gargoth looked at Marie and said, "No. I must protect your home from the creatures which besiege it. This is what gargoyles do."

"Please, Gargoth. You can't stay up there," her father continued. Just at that moment, some trick-or-treaters swung into sight around the corner of the street, happily laughing and swinging their candy bags. When they saw Katherine's parents out on the sidewalk, they ran towards them.

"Hey, Mr. Newberry!" said one of Katherine's school friends. Katherine's parents were frozen to the spot. They didn't know what to say. Katherine's mother shot a quick glance up at Gargoth, who was glowering down at the children standing around her.

"Uh, we just ran out of candy kids, sorry," said her father, thinking quickly. The children moaned and headed off down the street. While they were talking, Gargoth stood up as high as he could, and flapped his wings hard, in a threatening gesture, like an angry goose. Luckily, the children didn't notice him.

"Gargoth, please come down," Marie started again.

"We won't hand out any more candy, or anything. We'll all go into the backyard where we'll be safe, okay?"

Slowly, Gargoth nodded. "Yes, I will come down, if I do not need to protect your house any longer." He waddled to the side of the porch and climbed carefully down the ivy to the ground, where he waited quietly. Katherine's parents were quickly closing up the front of the house so it wouldn't attract any more trick-or-treaters. They took down the skeleton and picked up the leg-in-a-bag, removed the pumpkin and candy, and untied as much of the spider web thread as they could. Then they all traipsed into the backyard, the garden gate clicking behind them.

That was why her house was dark and empty-looking when Katherine arrived home with Sarah's mother an hour later. Usually her house was the last one to run out of candy, and the last pumpkin to go out for another year.

As she walked in the door, Katherine heard her mother saying, "He was protecting us, Hank. That's what gargoyles do. They ward off evil and danger. He was doing what he thought he was supposed to do."

"We could do that with a dog, Marie," her father answered sourly.

Katherine let the door click shut behind her.

Chapter Fifteen
What Gargoth Remembers

After his Halloween mishap, Gargoth became even more quiet and sullen. He thought he had been protecting this family from the ghosts and goblins of Halloween night, when instead he was just making them angry with him.

For several weeks he moped and did nothing but eat apples and lob the cores at the tree. It grew colder.

He didn't understand this place very well at all. It was confusing and strange. He didn't want to make his kind hosts angry with him again, so he pledged to himself that he wouldn't move from the backyard, no matter what he saw in the street.

Even rooted to the backyard, he did help them when he could. One day he was able to do them a very kind service. A terrible dog had chased Milly off the street and into the yard. Instead of stopping at the gate, the dog jumped the gate in hot pursuit of Milly and chased her right to the back fence. Milly, who as you know is a very smart cat, skidded to a halt behind Gargoth and stood to face the dog, arching her back and spitting. The dog growled and was ready to attack when he got the surprise of his life.

Gargoth, who had been still and watching, suddenly leaped to his feet and spread his wings wide, shrieking as loudly as he could in the dog's very surprised face.

That was the last they saw of that dog.

After that, Milly and Gargoth were fast friends. If her family was looking for her, they knew she was probably sitting under his pedestal, or occasionally sitting in his lap, allowing herself to be stroked by his cool, leathery claw.

There was also one night when Katherine could swear she heard men's voices in the backyard yelling, "Let's get out of here!" She smiled to herself and rolled over in her bed, secure knowing that Gargoth wouldn't let anyone near their house, especially if they were trying to climb over the back fence into the yard. He was better than a dog that way.

Gargoth tried his best to be good. He wanted to help the Newberry family, and in return, he hoped that Katherine would help him with the request he had made.

He wanted, more than anything, a chance to find a certain store. A store he had seen from the inside of a box as the lid was pried off. He had been lying in the box, hiding, when the lid was opened.

And she was taken away.

He could hardly bear to think of that moment and pushed it from his mind whenever it came to him.

Instead, Gargoth tried hard to remember what he could about the store. He knew it was quite small and dark and had a heavy scent of cinnamon candles. He also knew it was close to a busy road, and a great thundering machine went by frequently, which made the entire shop and all its contents quake as it passed. It was a large red machine with doors that opened and shut, letting people enter and leave as they pleased. He also knew that the person who owned the store was a tall woman with long curly red hair tied up in several scarves with beads. She wore long skirts and bangles, and she jangled and swished when she walked by the box he was hiding in.

Gargoth waited for his opportunity to talk to Katherine again about helping him find the store, but it was a long while before it came. And it was Katherine who brought it up.

During the weeks after Halloween, she had seen a change in her parents. A change in their entire lives. She had been thinking that she wanted to help her parents somehow. She saw how it upset them, not knowing how to help Gargoth on his way. She knew that they wanted to have a dinner party at Christmas time, but were afraid to invite people over in case Gargoth decided to defend their home again.

They were losing touch with their friends. The McDonalds were asking questions. And Katherine hadn't had any of her own friends over for a sleepover in ages.

It wasn't that they didn't like the little gargoyle. In fact, just the opposite: they really liked him. Which made the situation worse.

How do you get rid of a houseguest you don't really mind?

A very odd houseguest to be sure, but not an

obnoxious one. Not a mean or unfriendly one, particularly, but rather an interesting one with lots of stories to tell. In fact, she and her mother were beginning to really appreciate some of the finer points of having a gargoyle around. He never strayed from the yard, never asked to be let into the house, but if you bundled up and spent time with him in the yard under the cover of darkness, you would be richly rewarded with fabulous stories from the past.

Katherine came to understand that a rich, personal knowledge of history could come in very handy. One week, when Gargoth had overheard that Katherine was studying the great composer Mozart in history class, he grew very excited.

"Katherine! I didn't know that people still know about Mozart! Here, sit, I can tell you all that you need to know about Wolfgang Amadeus—I was one of his greatest admirers!"

Gargoth really was an expert. Katherine learned that he had first heard Mozart in Paris in the summer of 1778, when Mozart created a beautiful masterpiece called "Paris Symphony". (It's a long and interesting story, which you may read about some day, but you'll have to be satisfied with just a taste here). Gargoth sat entranced one hot July night on a nearby balcony as the beautiful music filled the air. Over that summer, Gargoth often perched himself near wherever the great composer was playing and listened blissfully. He had never heard anything like it, such pain and beauty combined together to create haunting musical perfection. Gargoth had been a very knowledgeable music fanatic ever since.

Gargoth and Katherine spent hours together in the backyard, discussing Mozart's life and musical practice. Katherine learned more than she ever wanted or needed to know about Mozart.

She got an "A" on that history project. Even Mrs. Glean was pleased!

Katherine learned that Gargoth had lived at one time or another in several towns in 17th and 18th century Europe, both in England and France. He told Katherine about the restoration of the great Notre Dame Cathedral in Paris, at that time the greatest church ever built. He had lived through the terrible French Revolution and once again, saw more terror and bloodshed than he cared to remember (which he mostly glossed over for Katherine's sake). He told her about the great plague that swept the European continent in 1665; so many people died that entire villages and towns were simply abandoned. He talked for hours about life in southern France in the 1700s (they kept a lot of bees, apparently). Katherine got the impression that life during those times was nearly unbearable, since it seemed from Gargoth's descriptions that people were really hungry and sick most of the time.

One night, after hearing yet another tale about a religious battle in England, Katherine finally had to blurt out, "Honestly, Gargoth, weren't there ever any good times? Didn't anyone ever have a good day, where they could just hang out and relax?"

He stopped and blinked at her, surprised. It took him a moment to accept the change in the course of their conversation, but when he understood what she was asking, he slowly smiled. "Of course, Katherine. There were many good things about living a long time ago." He paused, thinking for a moment.

"The air smelled better, for one thing." Here Katherine sighed, ready for another lecture. Gargoth had complained almost daily about the poor quality of the Toronto air, ever since he had arrived in their backyard. Katherine was so used to his complaining, she tuned him out and was no longer surprised if, right in the middle of a conversation, he stopped, wrinkled up his nose and started coughing. He hated the air and wondered often what it was doing to "one so young", meaning her.

He went on. "Food tasted better, too. These so-called apples barely have any flavour compared to the English apples of my early life. They were strong and tart, yet somehow sweet at the same time. There were lovely, clear blue skies and beautiful smells of hay and sweet clover in the summer." He closed his eyes, and Katherine could almost hear him sniffing the wind, remembering a time long ago and far away when the world did not smell like car exhaust and diesel fumes.

After a long pause, he finally added, "And the world was much, much quieter then, Katherine." As if to confirm the point, a car alarm suddenly started blaring on the street in front of the house. He flinched, hunching his shoulders a little, drawing his wings in tightly around himself. He glared toward the front of the house and wouldn't continue until the offending alarm stopped.

"I could stand on the church parapet on a deep

summer night and hear nothing but crickets, the wind in the long grass, and the trickle of the churchyard stream. Nothing but blissful silence, right until the first rooster crowed at sun-up."

Katherine wondered about that; she thought a serene and quiet world where the air smelled sweet and food tasted better sounded pretty good. But then there was all the bad stuff about religious persecution and starvation, no doctors, short life spans and constant illness, which she thought might make living in the past not so much fun, really.

One mid-December night, Katherine made up her mind. She would help Gargoth find the store he'd lost. She would help him, but they would have to be very careful. She didn't want her parents to find out. Or anyone else, for that matter.

After dinner that night, she went to visit him, which wasn't unusual, since either she or her mother or even her dad would once in a while, take an after-dinner snack out to him and say goodnight. It was becoming part of the family routine, deciding which one would check on him before bed.

He had taken a liking to hot chocolate, and this night Katherine was having some for herself, so she made him an extra mug. She told her parents she was going to say goodnight to Gargoth and stepped outside. The cold took her breath away and made the hot cup of chocolate suddenly look warm and inviting as steam furled up into the dark.

"Gargoth," she called quietly. "Gargoth?" There was a silence, then the bushes parted and out he stepped, regal as a small, fierce prince. Despite telling them he didn't feel the cold, Katherine noticed that he had taken to sleeping at night in the warmth of the bushes, especially when it was snowing.

She walked over to him and handed him the warm mug. He accepted it eagerly and took an enormous swig. He wiped his mouth then turned and grinned at her.

"Well, Katherine, I'm glad that you have made cocoa again. Thank you." They sat together beside the tree. Her parents had placed a small wooden bench near his pedestal so anyone could curl up and chat with him in comfort. Since her "A" in history, she and Gargoth had spent more and more time together.

"Gargoth, I've decided I will help you," she began. "I will help you find the store you are looking for."

There was a silence. Gargoth hid his face away from her for a moment, then turned to her with great, hot gargoyle tears coursing down his fat, leathery cheeks. Quietly he buried his little face in her coat. She could feel his hot tears hissing against the cool skin at her neck. It hurt. She gently pried him off her, concerned.

"Are you okay, Gargoth?" she asked, gazing intently into his face.

He took a deep breath and wiped his tears. "Okay? Okay, Katherine? Okay indeed! You have made me feel there is a...future. A way in the future for me..." He buried his face in her coat again for a moment, then turned away. He was making hiccoughing noises, too overcome to speak. Then he got up on his pedestal and danced an ancient jig, hooking his little claws under his wings and clicking his heels beneath his knees. Katherine giggled.

Once he had finished, he sat down again and caught his breath, saying, "You are very kind to me, Katherine. I know it has not been easy. I know that you had no choice but to accept me, and I regret..." he trailed off, suddenly sad. Her eyes followed his gaze to the flower patch, now empty and hoed to bare earth. Her parents had rid the yard of any remembrance of asters. He then let his eyes pass over the mended dwarf whose nose he had broken, so long ago it seemed now.

"I promise I will be good. I won't cause any problems for you, no matter what happens." And with that he extended his claw to Katherine. She carefully took it in her mittened hand, and they shook.

"Okay, Gargoth. We'll start looking for the store the first Wednesday after New Year's. I have piano lessons on Wednesdays, and I have to take the subway and the bus to my teacher's house, so I can put you in my bag after school and take you with me. We will have time to look at one store each week. It could take a long time. There are lots of stores in this city that might have gargoyles in them. Tell me everything you can remember about the one you are looking for."

So, as they sipped hot chocolate and sat in the cold night, she listened as the little gargoyle told her everything he could remember about the lost store.

When he was finished, she had a good idea where to start their search.

CHAPTER SIXTEEN
CHRISTMAS DAY STATUES

In no time, it seemed to Katherine, the first term of school was ended and it was time for Christmas holidays.

Christmas was always a fairly laid-back time for the Newberrys, pleasant and unhurried, with lots of friends to visit. They usually had one, large, exciting party for all their friends. Katherine was allowed to invite two friends, and they were always Sarah and Rubie.

This year was going to be a little different. Instead of the huge party they always had, Katherine's parents had decided they would tell everyone they couldn't have it this year because they were planning a long-awaited ski trip to Quebec. Katherine loved skiing, and although she would really miss the great party her parents always threw, she was really excited about the ski trip.

They were leaving on Boxing Day and had everything all ready and packed to go several days before, so they could laze around and enjoy Christmas day itself. They also wanted to say goodbye to Gargoth.

Christmas morning was clear and cold. Just as

though the snow gods were listening to every child's prayer on Christmas Eve, Christmas morning dawned with a fresh blanket of snow.

Katherine woke, sprang out of bed and looked out the window. It was her custom now to check on Gargoth from her bedroom window first thing each morning. Somehow he always knew when she was awake, and was waiting, smiling up at her when she peeked out. Christmas morning was no different. He was awake, gazing up at her window, waiting for her.

She waved excitedly at him, and he waved back.

But then she gasped and clapped her hands together in delight! Gargoth had been busy all night, making the most beautiful sculptures with the new snow!

As she looked over the backyard, she counted seventeen snow statues, each one a perfect gargoyle. Each was unique in its way, some were clearly female gargoyles, some were younger, older, grumpy or happy as Gargoth had made them.

One gargoyle was balanced perfectly on one toe, caught in a pirouette, just as Gargoth himself had been that terrible night when he'd stolen Katherine's shoes.

Another held a bouquet of what looked like asters.

Still another had her wings spread and was flying above a block of snow, suspended on a column of nearly invisible ice.

Each one was a beautiful work of art.

Katherine opened her window and called down to Gargoth, who was sitting perched on his pedestal, smoking his pipe. "Gargoth, they're beautiful!" She smiled at him.

He grinned back. "Good morning, Katherine! Merry Christmas!" he called.

"Merry Christmas, Gargoth!" she called and quickly shut the window. It really was a cold morning.

She ran down the hall to her parents' room and burst through the door, breathless. Both her parents, sleepy but happy, smiled up at her as she entered. Milly was curled up between them, asleep. They had already been up and made coffee and hot chocolate. Her mug was steaming on their bedside table. She jumped between them and said, "Merry Christmas, Mom! Merry Christmas, Dad!"

"Did you see the statues?" she asked, after sipping her delicious cocoa.

Her mother was smiling. For the first time in a long while, she looked really happy.

"Yes, they're really beautiful. I think we should take pictures of them so we can keep them around forever," she said.

Soon it was time for presents. After each Newberry family member had opened his or her gift, and after a huge breakfast of Froot Loops (forbidden the rest of the year), pancakes and maple syrup, the Newberrys put their warmest coats and boots on over their pajamas, and carried out their presents for Gargoth.

Gargoth was sitting beneath the sculpture of the beautiful flying gargoyle, smoking his pipe. He looked calm and peaceful, almost happy.

"Hello, Newberrys. I hope you enjoy the snow sculptures I have made for you."

"Oh, they're beautiful, Gargoth. Thank you!" said

Katherine and her mother, almost together. Katherine's father simply said "The statues are beautiful, Gargoth." He still hadn't been able to understand when Gargoth spoke, although sometimes he thought he caught a word here and there.

Gargoth stood up and came over to the family. He waved his arms over the seventeen beautiful statues, and said, "I have created a world of friends I will never have." He pointed at a squat, very sturdy and youthful-looking sculpture with fat cheeks. "A young friend perhaps. I will name him Andrathene."

"And that one I will name Magra." This time he waved toward an older-looking gargoyle with a grandmotherly face.

He turned and gazed up at the flying gargoyle. Up close, Katherine could see that she was sweet looking, her face wasn't wrinkled and crumpled like the others. She had a small pouch at her side, just like Gargoth's.

"Who is that one?" asked Katherine, pointing at the flying gargoyle.

Gargoth looked at her steadily. He sighed. "Her name is Ambergine. But she is no one."

Katherine and Gargoth looked at each other for a moment, and she knew he was lying. This was a sculpture of the gargoyle he was hoping to find, the only real gargoyle in the entire group of imaginary friends. She was the gargoyle that they would soon be searching for in every candle and comic book store in Toronto.

She tactfully changed the subject. "Um, Mom! What do you have for Gargoth?"

"Oh! Right!" her mother said. "Look Gargoth, these are Cellini apples shipped from a hillside in southern Italy—they are an ancient variety once cultivated by the Greeks and Romans. They are difficult to grow, but they are exquisite. I had to sample one for myself! I hope you like them!" She placed a huge basket overflowing with the most beautiful, glowing apples Katherine had ever seen.

They smelled like heaven. Gargoth picked one up gently in his claw and took a long sniff of its rich, sweet scent. "Oh, they will be delicious. Thank you, Mother Newberry."

It was Katherine's turn. She brought her gift out from behind her back and held out a new, oversized cocoa cup for Gargoth. "This is so we can enjoy long chats over hot chocolate together, and you don't run out first!" she said. Gargoth seemed really touched and turned the cocoa cup around in his hands, holding it up close to his face. It had a checkered pattern and wavy lines on it, which seemed to intrigue him. He looked at it for a long time, finally thanking Katherine in a hushed voice.

Then Katherine's father stepped forward, not understanding a word, but seeing it was his turn. He dropped a large pouch into Gargoth's claw. On opening it, Gargoth made a strange noise, which sounded like a gargoyle being taken by surprise (an odd sound to be sure, but not an unpleasant one).

"Ah, Father Newberry, you honour me with fine English tobacco, my favourite," he said, clearly touched once again.

Gargoth surprised Katherine's father with a genuine smile and a handshake. (Shaking Gargoth's claw was actually a little dangerous, it was sharp!)

The Newberrys were very happy. If anyone were looking into their little backyard, they would have seen a very loving family gathered around a gargoyle, who looked just like he loved them back.

And a very smart cat watching everything from the warmth of indoors.

Chapter Seventeen
The Promise

Katherine enjoyed the family ski trip more than she had imagined she would. They stayed in a ski chalet, right on the mountain, and kept their skis outside the front door in a snow bank. When they wanted to ski, they just walked outside and stepped into them.

There were pine trees growing right outside her bedroom window, and they smelled so heavenly that every evening she opened her window so she could enjoy them all night long.

Her room had its own fireplace and a huge window looking out onto the forest. Her parents' room was even bigger than hers and had a jacuzzi big enough for a football team.

It was very luxurious. It was perfect, in fact. Only once did Katherine think of Gargoth. On their last day, she was skiing into the main chalet, when she happened to look up. There on top of the old building was a gargoyle. She was so surprised, she almost fell face first into the snow. When she righted herself, she stood and watched the gargoyle for a few moments. But she quickly realized it was simply a stone gargoyle, just a statue on the roof, not a real living creature like Gargoth.

She felt a pang and suddenly realized how much she had come to consider him part of the family. Just then her mother skied up. They looked at the gargoyle together for a while.

"I wonder what Gargoth would look like on skis?" her mother said.

The image was so hysterical that Katherine laughed herself into a fit of hiccoughing. Once she caught her breath, she challenged her mother to a race down the big hill.

The next day the family returned home. Gargoth seemed genuinely pleased to see them. It had been warmer in Toronto than on the ski slopes, and many of the statues Gargoth had created on Christmas Eve were starting to melt. They looked ghoulish and spooky, melting slowly away, with sadly drooping wings and drooling fangs. Gargoth didn't seem to notice.

School started the next day, and this was the first week of Katherine's piano lessons for the second term. If she had forgotten their agreement, Gargoth hadn't. At the first opportunity, he reminded her of her promise from a few weeks before. After dinner on Sunday night, Katherine took out a mug of hot chocolate in the new huge, checkered mug she had given him for Christmas.

"We will start looking for her this week, then?" he reminded her, as soon as they were alone in the backyard.

"Yes, Gargoth," she said. "I promised. But I have to

say I'm not really happy about it. It's a lot of sneaking around, and I don't like to do that behind my parents' backs. I really feel like I should tell them." She sat in the bench beside his pedestal and brushed some snow off the back of the unicorn's mane.

"No, Katherine. Please, I promise all will be well."

He was so earnest that she sighed and said, "Fine. But if there are any problems, if I'm late for piano even once, we'll have to tell them and find another way."

"Don't worry, Katherine. It will be fine." Gargoth delicately tipped up his mug to get his final sip of hot chocolate (despite what you might think, gargoyles are actually very tidy eaters) and grinned at her.

She went inside a few moments later, still not feeling great about the adventure she was about to undertake, traipsing through Toronto's subway with a supposed-to-be-inanimate creature talking to her from her backpack. But she felt she might just be able to help him find the gargoyle he was searching for, and if he did find her, Katherine felt certain he would be able to leave her family, leave her backyard, and carry on with his own life.

And that's what they all wanted, wasn't it, Katherine thought? For him to get unstuck from their lives, and get on with his own? She also knew her parents had grown fond of him, but she knew they were saddened by the changes in their lives. No parties. No friends to visit. No beautiful flowers. She missed having her own friends over for sleepovers. And it was getting harder and harder to come up with reasons not to invite people over.

No matter how she looked at it, Katherine had to admit it was difficult having a gargoyle living in her backyard.

Monday morning dawned. The family quickly returned to their pre-Christmas routines. It always surprised Katherine how fast the events of the holidays became a dream-like memory.

She was happy to see her friends at school again. They all talked about what they had been doing over the holidays. She had a lot of fun telling everyone what the ski trip had been like.

All too soon, Wednesday morning arrived, and with a faint sense of dread, Katherine realized that today was the day. Her mother waved out the back door to Gargoth, then she and Katherine got into the car, and off they drove to school.

From the back seat, Katherine said as casually as she could, "So, piano starts again tonight, Mom."

"Oh, yes! I forgot! Do you remember how to get to Elaine's?" her mother asked absentmindedly.

"Uh-huh. Take the bus down Christie to the subway, then go east to Castle Frank, then north one street to her house. I remember. You'll pick me up at six o'clock outside her house, right?"

"Yes. I'll be there. And please remember to call me when you get there. Promise?"

"Yeah, Mom, don't worry, I'll call." Katherine bit her lip, kissed her mother goodbye, then jumped out of the car and bounded into the school. She was beginning to wonder how on earth she was going to get home, get Gargoth into her backpack, then dash downtown and back up to her piano lesson on time.

It wouldn't be easy. The night before, she and Gargoth had agreed that he would be waiting at the back fence. She thought she could run home after school, take the shortcut to their backyard down the lane, then he could leap over the fence, and she'd save at least five minutes off going the long way to the front door.

The day at school seemed impossibly long and slow. But finally it ended, without mishap. At last three-thirty came, and Katherine took off like a shot. Her friend Rubie ran across the school field to try to catch her, but Katherine pretended not to hear her and kept running. The last thing she wanted was to explain why she needed to get home really quickly today.

It worked perfectly. The day was clear and cold, but most of the snow had melted, so Katherine could run as fast as she wanted over the sidewalks without slipping. She had her big yellow canvas backpack on, and she hoped Gargoth would fit. Try as she might, she hadn't been able to convince him to get in the night before, just to make sure there was enough room for him.

She smiled, in spite of herself. "Such pride!" she thought.

She arrived at the back fence at exactly 3:42. "Twelve minutes! That's pretty good for two kilometres!" she thought. Then she whistled softly, as they had agreed.

A second later, she heard a loud thud beside her. There was Gargoth, lying in the muddy lane, looking very upset.

"You're late, Katherine! And I'm all muddy and wet!" he complained.

She sighed. "Get in Gargoth, and be quiet." She

squatted down, and the little gargoyle clambered up onto her back, pulled himself over the rim of the sturdy canvas backpack and slid in, head first.

He grunted, then Katherine had an uncomfortable sensation as he wriggled and righted himself to rest on his large feet.

"Uh, Gargoth," she began, as she stood up and adjusted the straps of the backpack to allow for more room for him, "would you mind turning the other way. Your, uh, claws are digging into my back."

Gargoth grunted again, and after a few minutes of squirming and snorting and, Katherine was sure, quite unnecessary sighing, he had turned himself inside the backpack so his back was against Katherine's back. She had to admit that scaly wings rubbing against her back were only slightly more comfortable than pointy claws sticking into her ribs.

She had been walking all the while. "Next week, we bring a soft towel for you to lean against," Katherine whispered over her back. She was walking down Bloor Street now and didn't want people to see her whispering into her backpack.

All she heard in response from Gargoth was a soft snort. He was asleep!

"That's probably good," she thought. "I don't have to worry about him talking to me on the subway."

She reached the subway entrance, paid her student fare, then waited on the eastbound platform for the next train. No one could possibly know what was inside her backpack, but she was nervous and jumpy all the same.

And Gargoth, small as he was, was beginning to feel quite heavy. Katherine hoped no one would notice that her backpack was snoring.

Chapter Eighteen
The First Store

Judging by Gargoth's description of the store and the large red "locomotion machine," as he called it, Katherine had decided that they should start looking in the stores along the streetcar route of Toronto's Queen Street East. The area was full of antique shops, comic book stores and strange little boutiques which were an odd mixture of both. There were plenty to choose from, so to pick the first store, she simply ran her finger down the list in the phone book and stopped randomly at Crystal Knights; she liked the sound of it. That would be the first store they would visit.

Katherine had ridden in peace on the subway, since Gargoth slept the entire trip. When she transferred to the Queen streetcar, he stirred a little but still did not wake up.

She found Crystal Knights without any trouble, and finally had no choice but to wake Gargoth. She was really nervous about doing this, since gargoyles are notoriously grumpy when you wake them up from a sound sleep. Luckily, there was a bench right outside the store, where she sat heavily and took off her backpack. Gently she shook the bag, saying, "Gargoth, we're here! Wake up!" It took a few shakes and whispers before she heard the familiar snarl and snap. She was glad this was a sturdy canvas backpack.

Once Gargoth was wide awake and no longer snarling at her, Katherine re-shouldered the backpack and went toward the store. Her heart was pounding. Gargoth had promised to keep still but insisted that his head peek out the top of the backpack, so he wouldn't miss a thing.

As Katherine opened the door, a little bell tinkled their arrival to the proprietor working among the boxes in the storeroom at the back. The place was warm and smelled like incense.

"Just a minute!" a happy, loud woman's voice called. Katherine could feel Gargoth's body tense behind her. "Katherine! This seems right! It smells right! It looks right! And it's a woman here!" Gargoth was practically yelling at her.

"Be quiet! You promised!" Katherine snapped over her shoulder, but she had to stop because the unseen owner had just appeared, beaming at them over the counter.

A short lady with thick glasses and frizzy hair smiled down at her. "Hello!" she said pleasantly. "Can I help you?"

Here we go, thought Katherine. "Um, yes, please," she said. "I have a gargoyle here, and we are looking for a matching one. My mother really loves this one and wants to try and find another one just like it. Have you seen anything like this one before?"

The lady-owner bustled happily around the counter

and peered into the backpack at Gargoth. "Please, Gargoth," Katherine breathed to herself, "be good!"

He was. As good as gold. He stayed perfectly rigid and still while the lady looked him over, very closely.

"Oh, isn't he beautiful? Can I take him out?" she asked. Katherine froze. She hadn't thought of that. Of course, the owner would want to see him and touch him! "Okay, I guess...he's pretty precious! Be careful!"

The lady carefully took hold of Gargoth and lifted him from the backpack. She placed him on the counter, and she and Katherine stood back to admire him. Katherine was very worried, but extremely impressed with Gargoth's statue-like demeanour. He really did look like a perfect little gargoyle statue, grumpy and lifelike. But not necessarily real.

There was a long silence. "He really is remarkable, isn't he? I mean, you'd swear he's alive!" She was just going to touch Gargoth again when the front door bell tinkled. A delivery man came through the door with a hand-trolley overflowing with boxes marked "Skulls/candles".

"Just one moment, dear." The lady turned her back to Katherine and Gargoth for a moment, and Gargoth took the opportunity to sullenly stick his tongue out at her as she retreated. Then he shook his head sadly at Katherine. This wasn't the right store.

While the lady was busy with the delivery man, Katherine took off her backpack and carefully stuffed Gargoth back in. It would have been easier if he'd climbed in himself, but of course, they couldn't risk that.

The lady came back to them just as Katherine was

strapping her backpack closed. "You know, I've never seen another gargoyle like him, dear. He's really one of a kind, don't you think?" She smiled sweetly at Katherine.

"Yes." Katherine smiled weakly back at her. "Yes, I'm quite sure he really is."

Feeling sadder than she thought possible, Katherine left the store and headed back to the bus stop. She looked at her watch: 4:25! She'd have to hurry to make it to piano on time. She started at a trot. Gargoth was perfectly silent behind her, although he was being bumped and banged against her body mercilessly. She was sure she was getting bruised. Although he wasn't very big, Gargoth was sturdy and pointy where he bumped against your body.

"I'm really sorry, Gargoth," Katherine panted over her shoulder as she ran. "You couldn't really expect the first store we tried to be the right one, though. Could you? I mean there are dozens of stores just like that one, near the street car lines. It could take us months to check them all, Gargoth."

There was only silence behind her. And the occasional sniffle.

Katherine dashed to the Broadview bus, then ran all the way from the Castle Frank station to her piano lesson with just five minutes to spare.

As Katherine entered the timeless luxury of her piano teacher's house, and the big oak door to the panelled piano room slid with a "shush" behind her, she realized she hadn't thought of something: what was Gargoth going to do while she had her piano lesson?

Elaine, her teacher, was waiting at the piano bench for her. "Hello, Katherine! Just in time. How was your holiday?" she asked, happy to see her student.

Suddenly aching with worry and tired from her run, Katherine said, "Oh, sorry, Elaine! I just have to call my mother!" She bolted back out into the hallway, slid the door shut behind her and picked up the phone on the table. As she was dialing her mother, she whispered to her backpack, "Gargoth, you've got to be really, really quiet during my lesson. Can you breathe in there?"

Gargoth whispered back. "I will be quiet as long as you play well. I cannot endure poor piano playing." Katherine caught a note of a sniff in Gargoth's tone, just as though he was reminding her that he had listened to Mozart himself play, one of the greatest pianists the world has ever known.

Katherine sighed. There was nothing for it. Gargoth would have to listen to her piano lesson and stay perfectly quiet. Katherine left a message on her mother's voicemail at work, propped her backpack up outside the sliding oak door and walked in.

"Katherine, are you okay?" Elaine asked her. She seemed a little worried.

Katherine really liked her piano teacher. She was a grandmotherly lady who dressed beautifully and who really enjoyed teaching kids how to read music. She'd been a piano teacher for thirty-five years, but unlike many others, she had never grown tired of the job. And she picked great music for Katherine to learn.

"Yes, yes, I'm fine. Thanks. Just a little tired." She smiled.

"Where's your music then?" Elaine asked, expectantly.

Music. Oh no, it was in her backpack! "Oh, yes, how silly of me! I'll just get it." She slid open the heavy oak door one final time and looked over at her backpack. To her dismay, there was her music sticking out the half-closed top, clutched in an all-too familiar claw.

She snatched it and slid the door closed once again. Luckily, Elaine hadn't seen her music waving above her backpack in the hallway. She could breathe again.

Sadly, this wasn't Katherine's best lesson. And Elaine didn't want to say anything to Katherine, but she was sure that every time Katherine hit a wrong note, which for some reason was rather frequent, her backpack sneezed. Or grunted. Or maybe it made a noise like the wind in the leaves.

They were both relieved when the lesson was finally over and Katherine's mother beeped the car horn from the driveway.

"Thanks, Elaine. Sorry, I didn't really practice much over the holidays. I think I'll be better next week. Bye!"

Katherine grabbed her bag and dashed out the door to find her mother waiting. She was careful to stash her backpack in the trunk for the ride home, and she didn't really care if certain individuals found it cold and uncomfortable back there.

Luckily, when they got home it was dark, and Katherine had enough time to sneak Gargoth into the backyard before her mother checked on him.

Katherine didn't speak to Gargoth or even venture

into the backyard for several days after that adventure. She was too shaken.

CHAPTER NINETEEN
CANDLES BY DAYE

The next week, Katherine and Gargoth agreed on two things: he would stay hidden in the backpack during the entire time he was in each store, and he would wait outside in the bushes during her piano lesson.

Making the first change was easy. They just needed to make some adjustments to the backpack. Katherine made two eyeholes in the fabric so Gargoth could peek out and check each store without being seen.

The second change was much harder and more dangerous. Each time Katherine arrived, breathless, at Elaine's house, she would take off her backpack and let Gargoth scramble out into the bushes by the front door. They had some very close calls, including one awful night when Elaine had been watching from the window and insisted on checking the bushes carefully for what she thought was a large "rodent".

Luckily she hadn't seen too much, most importantly where the "rodent" had come from, and Gargoth was able to hide from her in the bushes.

Getting him back in the backpack after the lesson was just as difficult, but since it was dark by the time her mother arrived, Gargoth could usually climb into it unseen. He was actually getting quite good at jumping onto Katherine and into the backpack as she bent next to the bush he was hiding in, pretending to tie her shoe.

It was a difficult time for them both. It was made even more difficult by the fact that they were having no luck finding the right store. But neither of them gave up. Winter was slowly turning to spring, but somehow neither Elaine nor Katherine's mother figured out that the little gargoyle was hiding in Katherine's backpack.

Each Wednesday, their adventure was the same. Katherine would rush home, pick up Gargoth, rush onto the subway and the streetcar, then dash into a store that turned out to be the wrong one. The only good thing was that the adjustments to the backpack worked perfectly. Gargoth was kept hidden and safe during each visit, and they didn't have to endure the terror of nosy store owners trying to touch him.

They had been to every store along a good portion of Queen Street: Dungeons and Dragoons, Knyghtes and Ladies, Comix Culture, Gifties and Ghoulies, Starlite, Dragon's Breath and several more. Katherine was a little disheartened at the pages of stores listed under "candles" and "novelties" in the Toronto phonebook. There were dozens and dozens of them. Who knew so many people wanted to buy skull-shaped candles, hanging bead curtains and healing chime balls?

Each store was essentially the same as the last. The door chimes tinkled when they entered. They were hit with the aroma of incense or candles, sometimes nearly overpowering them. They wandered up to the counter and faced some variation of an owner, tall and thin, short and chubby, angry, happy, frizzy haired, with or without glasses. The storeowners all became a version of one another after a while, each looking vaguely like the last.

Finally, after ten weeks of looking, Katherine and Gargoth were beginning to give up hope. It was early March, and the city was starting to smell once again like early spring.

This particular Wednesday, Katherine was trudging into yet another store, this one called Candles by Daye. By now it only took a few moments for Gargoth to let her know if they had found the right place. They had worked out a quiet, secret code which, unfortunately for Katherine, was a system of jabs from Gargoth. If the place was wrong, Gargoth jabbed her once (as gently as he could) on her left side. Theoretically, if it was the right store, he would jab her once on the right side, but this of course hadn't happened yet. Needless to say, Katherine's left side had developed a permanent bruise, which she was beginning to doubt would ever clear up.

As she entered this particular store, a streetcar rumbled to a stop on Queen Street behind her. She could feel Gargoth tense up in the backpack behind her.

"It's okay, Gargoth," she whispered. "It's just a streetcar, you know that."

As she entered the store, Katherine was immediately hit with a heavy scent of cinnamon.

"I'll never light another candle as long as I live," she thought as she wandered up to the counter.

The little store and its entire contents shook as the streetcar outside pulled away. Dust puffed from between the shelves and shelves of self-help and yoga books. An assortment of small ornaments quivered dangerously. The gentle song of dozens of jiggling chimes and healing balls filled the air.

Katherine took a moment to look around. It was a very small, dark store, and as far as she could tell, it was packed with dragons, fairies, dwarves, and all manner of mythical creatures.

Except, of course, like every other store they had visited recently, there were no gargoyles.

She sighed. "Here we go again," she whispered, but Gargoth did not answer. She could feel him squirming behind her. "Keep still, you're hurting me," she begged.

The store appeared to be deserted. She rang the bell on the counter. In what seemed a mind-bending flash of speed, a tall woman with long, curly red hair bounced from the back of the store to the front in one leap. She had been bending over a box of knick-knacks, and Katherine hadn't seen her.

Katherine pulled back in surprise. She had to bend back to catch the full height of the woman, she was so tall.

But very friendly. Perhaps a little too friendly. "Hello! I'm Cassandra, can I help you?" She smiled a giantess smile at Katherine, who was so overcome for a moment she could only stand and stare.

She felt a painful jab in her back (in a rather central spot near her spine, so as not to cause any confusion), which reminded her why she was there.

"Oh, uh," she stammered. Another jab helped clear her mind and find her voice.

Slightly annoyed now, Katherine began the line she had said so often she could recite it in her sleep.

"Um, yes, please," she said. "I'm looking for a gargoyle. My mother is a collector, and she is looking for a very specific one. Do you have any?"

Cassandra looked thoughtful for a moment. "Actually, we did have a gargoyle until recently." Cassandra trailed off, looking more closely at Katherine. "Could you describe it? How big, facial expression, anything?"

"Well, he's about this big," Katherine showed Cassandra Gargoth's approximate size with her hands. "He's got small, leathery wings and a pouch on one side. He looks kind of gloomy. Oh, and he's sitting down."

"Hmm. I don't think I have anything like that, but I'll just go into the back and see. I'll be right back," the woman said and swooshed away, her long skirts making a soft sound like a summer breeze.

Katherine jumped. Gargoth had given her a particularly hard jab. She gasped and whispered, "What are you doing that for? Stop it!"

Before she knew it, Gargoth had clambered out of the bag and hopped onto the counter, clearly forgetting that her right side was for jabbing if the store felt "right".

"This is it! This is it, Katherine!" he shouted. "This is the place. It is the right woman, I know it. It smells right. It is close enough to the streetcar. I…" Gargoth froze. Cassandra had swooshed back into sight.

He was standing, frozen, with his claws gesticulating wildly and his mouth wide open. He looked crazed. And very much alive.

Katherine held her breath. For what seemed like hours, Cassandra stood and stared at Gargoth, who was doing his best to look like a statue.

Katherine broke the silence uncomfortably. "Here is a version of what my mother is looking for, except like I said, the one she is looking for is sitting down."

Cassandra nodded slowly at Katherine, then moved closer to Gargoth. Slowly she reached out and stroked his wing, then his head, then his back. She too seemed to be holding her breath.

"He is beautiful," she said quietly. She spoke like someone talking about a very rare and expensive painting, or an antique. Katherine's parents loved to watch antique shows on television, and she had overheard this reverential tone used by antique dealers speaking in the presence of an unusual and extremely rare find.

Cassandra stood before Gargoth for a moment, then turned away. It seemed to Katherine that she had to rip her eyes from him, and although she wasn't absolutely sure, Katherine thought she may have had tears in them. Cassandra strode toward the back room. "I'll be right back."

While she was gone, neither Gargoth nor Katherine wasted any time getting Gargoth back into the backpack, and safely hidden.

Cassandra returned, holding a picture. She didn't seem surprised that the little gargoyle was back in the backpack. She thrust the picture at Katherine. "I did have a gargoyle amazingly like him," she said.

Katherine looked closely at the picture. Cassandra looked closely at Katherine. Here was an exact replica of the Christmas-day statue Gargoth had made; the female gargoyle flying over a block of ice, the one he had called "Ambergine". She looked sweeter and softer, somehow, than Gargoth, but also very similar. She even had a pouch at her side, just like him. In the picture she was sitting with her claws tucked under her chin, looking funny and morose at the same time.

"Where is she now?" asked Katherine softly, raising her eyes to Cassandra's.

Cassandra moved closer and bent down before her, so her large face was level with Katherine's.

"I'm sorry," she said quietly, "but she disappeared a few days ago." She paused, then spoke so quietly that Katherine had to draw even closer to hear her. "I think she flew away."

Chapter Twenty
If Only...

Katherine stared at Cassandra for a long time. "Flew away?" she finally managed to ask.

"Yes," said Cassandra. "I put her outside on the first fine day of spring last week. She sat in the sun all afternoon long, but she was gone when I went to collect her."

"How do you know she wasn't stolen?" asked Katherine. Cassandra smiled deeply.

"Because I know she could fly. I caught her flying one night, when she thought I wasn't here. I was in the back, counting the dragons, when I heard a crash out front. I quietly put my head through the curtains, and there she was, flying from the counter top to the book shelf and back. She really wasn't very good at it, though," she added thoughtfully. "She kept crashing into things."

Katherine didn't know what to say.

Cassandra went on. "Even before I knew she could fly, I knew that she was different from the other gargoyles I've had here. I mean, she looked real, for one thing. And she was light, and her eyes were alive. There was another one like her in the box, but he was sent to The Golden Nautilus. As soon as I saw your gargoyle, I knew it was him. He's quite loud, isn't he? I saw him through the curtains jumping around on the countertop. Believe me, I would have kept them if only..."

"If you'd known they were alive?" Katherine finished.

"Yes. I would have kept them happy and together. I never would have separated them. I'm sorry." Cassandra looked sadly at Katherine. "I think your gargoyle is lovely. Let him know I'll keep my eyes open for her. Keep in touch with me, I'll let you know if I see her." Cassandra handed Katherine a Candles By Daye business card with her number and her name, Cassandra Daye, printed on it.

Katherine thanked Cassandra and walked sadly out of the store. Cassandra watched her go.

The day was dark and drizzly. A streetcar came by and splashed Katherine, but she hardly noticed.

As she walked slowly along Queen Street, not caring if she was late for piano, she could barely bring herself to talk to Gargoth. The backpack was very still.

Finally, as she wandered onto the Broadview bus to take her up to Danforth and the Castle Frank station, she said, "Gargoth, I'm really, really sorry. If she flew away, maybe we can still find her?"

Gargoth said nothing. What was there to say? He sniffled and stayed quiet, digging his way further down into the backpack. Katherine didn't try to speak to him again.

Her piano lesson was a disaster. Luckily, it was the final lesson for the term.

Unlike other Wednesday nights, Katherine kept her backpack on her knee on the drive home and hugged it gently all the way.

CHAPTER TWENTY-ONE
Night Flight

Finally, spring arrived in the city. Slush disappeared, and lost mittens were found. Children were liberated from suffocating scarves and down coats and were released to the freedom of spring jackets and caps.

Gargoth hadn't been himself since their visit to Candles by Daye. He was grumpy, sad and humourless, so that even Milly kept her distance from him.

But there were still miracles to be had. As the sun returned the Newberry backyard to life, an amazing transformation had taken place over the winter. And it seemed that Gargoth had a large part to play in the new landscape of the yard.

For there, in the old aster patch, which no one could bring themselves to talk about or look at, there were sprouting the very beginnings of a new patch of flowers. And if her parents knew anything about asters, these were going to be spectacular!

But there was more. In the very centre of the yard, nestled between the unicorn fountain and the dwarf patch, was an astonishingly beautiful tree. It was an apple tree, grown from the seeds of the rare Italian

Cellini apples Katherine's mother had given to Gargoth as a Christmas gift.

The young tree looked glorious, with golden boughs and sweet-smelling bark. Katherine and her parents couldn't believe it. It was a real miracle that this tree, coddled and coached to good health in the warmth of the Italian sunshine, could be made to grow in the cold, dark Canadian winter in downtown Toronto.

"How, Gargoth? How did you do it?" her mother asked the morning the tree was discovered pushing up through the turf at an amazing, even magical, pace.

Gargoth smiled a wise, gentle smile. "It will grow quickly, Mother Newberry. And hopefully you will no longer need to feed me so many buckets of apples. I will have my own supply."

"And the asters, Gargoth. How?" Katherine's mother allowed the words to die on her lips.

Gargoth just looked down and said quietly, "I hope you will forgive me, Mother Newberry. I hope the new patch will grow and bring you awards once again."

Katherine's mother bent forward and kissed Gargoth on his leathery head. He looked surprised, then smiled.

"They are not much, perhaps, but they are my gifts to you in the coming of the new season."

Spring was truly beautiful that year. Gargoth, though a sadder and perhaps gentler gargoyle, remained with them in their backyard. His life with them took on a regular, day-to-day rhythm. The Newberrys even managed a summer barbecue to celebrate Katherine's thirteenth birthday, and Gargoth stayed quietly out of sight in the bushes by the back fence. No one even suspected he was there.

In time, the glorious Italian apple tree did win awards for the Newberrys, as did the amazing new patch of New England Asters. Their neighbours, the McDonalds, were once again regular dinner guests.

Life returned to normal, or as normal as it was going to be with a gargoyle living in their yard, even a good-as-gold gargoyle like Gargoth.

But that is not the end of the story.

One fine summer night after the family had enjoyed a barbecue with friends in the Newberry's backyard, Gargoth sat on his pedestal and smoked his pipe with Milly curled up on his lap. Gargoth looked up to the heavens then down at the cat.

The stars shone brightly. The moon was just beginning to rise behind the CN Tower, bathing the city in a cool, silver glow.

"Well, Milly my friend," Gargoth said to the cat as he scratched her gently between the ears, "I guess that's the end to another fine day." He thought about the party the Newberrys had had that night, and the happy sound of friends and neighbours chatting nearby as he hid quietly in the bushes by the fence. As he thought of these things, he nodded off to sleep, snuffling and dropping his head slowly onto his chest.

As Milly looked up into his face purring, something in the night sky caught her attention, right at the edge of her sharp vision.

She stiffened and sat up. She wagged her tail and growled softly, staring all the while straight up into the sky above the city. She jumped down from Gargoth's lap and up onto the fence.

Milly stared and stared, like a statue-cat transfixed on the top of the fence.

There, up in the heavens, silvery in the moonlight caught against the clouds, was the tiny outline of a gargoyle, flying over the city, circling, circling, and looking carefully for the one she had lost.

She knows Gargoth is there, waiting for her, somewhere in the vast city below. It will take much time and effort, and another story you may read one day, but she won't give up: she knows she will find him. And you and I know he will be there for her, waiting among friends.

EpiloGue

It is many years from now.

One summer day, a young boy is walking in an old English churchyard. It is a very pretty place, surrounded by rolling green hills and chestnut trees. A small, sweet river runs beside the church courtyard. An ancient stone lion looks to the west, his stone mane blazing in the sun. His left ear is broken off and lies in the grass at his feet.

The boy and his family are visiting the ruins of an old church, long abandoned now. The boy is wandering quietly by himself in the apple orchard, looking back up at the church and thinking about what it would have been like to live there, so long ago.

Suddenly, a small scurrying catches his eye. He looks more closely, steadying himself against a tree, and for a moment he is sure he sees two little figures disappear behind the church parapet. He sees the outline of a wing, a leathery head, and maybe a claw.

Stranger still, just as he is sure he imagined it, an apple core lands in the grass near him, followed by a trill of laughter.

It is an unusual but happy sound, like a language he is just beginning to forget. Or like the wind rustling in the winter leaves.

He turns to go and finds himself smiling in the warm sunshine.

Philippa Dowding wrote her first novel when she was nine and has worked at the craft of writing ever since. As a copywriter, her work has won several industry awards for magazines as varied as *Maclean's*, *Chatelaine*, *Today's Parent* and *The Beaver*.

The Gargoyle In My Yard was inspired by an experience in a strange little antique store. She looked up an ancient stairway and saw a small gargoyle statue on each step. When she turned away and looked back, each statue seemed to have moved. What began as a bedtime story for her children turned into this book.

Philippa lives in Toronto with her husband and two children. She can be contacted at pdowding.com.

A Note on Gargoyles

Gargoyles are everywhere. You'll find them looking down on you in big cities and small towns. They may be funny animals, unusual people, or frightening, mystical creatures.

First created in Europe in the middle ages, true gargoyles were water downspouts on medieval buildings. The word "gargoyle" comes from the French "gargouille" which means "to gargle"—it's the sound you'll hear when water spouts through a gargoyle's mouth. Look up—you never know where you'll find a gargoyle!